MW01612898

Emperor Dad
by Henry Melton

Wire Rim Books
Hutto, Texas

This is a work of fiction. Names, events, locations, if they exist elsewhere, are used here fictitiously and any resemblence to real persons, places, or events is entirely coincidental.

Emperor Dad © 2003 by Henry Melton

Printing History
First Edition July 2007
Second Edition May 2008

ISBN: 978-0-9802253-4-1

(First Edition published under ISBN: 978-0-6151-5357-5)

Website of Henry Melton:
http://HenryMelton.com/

Cover art by Wes Hartman

Wire Rim Books
http://WireRimBooks.com/

Contents

Special thanks to the review crew; Debra Andrews, Jim Dunn, Linda Elliott, Colleen LaSoya, Alan McConnell and Tom Stock.

For Thomas

Plan B

1

Heavy raindrops rattled the metal roof of the storage building like spent shotgun pellets. The approaching thunderstorm had turned the sky to the north black, traced with branching lightning. Shaking like a drum head, the walls of the twelve by twenty foot building vibrated from a close thunderstrike—a *ker-crack!* that came from the *inside.* Seconds later, mellowed by distance, that very same ker-crack echoed from two miles away.

And then, gushing from every crack and seam, a flood of chocolate brown water spilled out. Hundreds of gallons of dirty river water knocked the door open, showing the computers inside.

A man backed his way through the door, wading through the flow.

Bob Hill, his eyes wide with panic, dragged the limp, soaked body of his son James out into the yard. Setting him down in the mud, he felt for a pulse. It was there, but very weak. Blood was oozing from a laceration on the boy's head.

He's bleeding. That's a good sign. In the daylight, his skin was pale. *Extreme blood loss.* Bob face was twisted, barely able to contain a cry of pain. *I've got to get him to a hospital.*

Ignoring the flickering from the shed as the power shorted out, he lifted the boy—a young man—and stumbled around the house to the driveway. He strapped James into the back seat of the Jeep Cherokee and as lightning struck the ridge just above the fence line of their five-acre home, he grabbed the cell phone.

The wheels spit gravel as he raced out the driveway.

"Williamson County 9-1-1 Emergency Services. What is the emergency?"

Bob fishtailed around the corner onto the county road, belatedly flipping the four-wheel drive lever into play. The road was wet and getting slippery.

"My son's been in an automobile accident."

Bob's mind raced, giving the operator a story just good enough. Not the real one of course. That one began several weeks before.

2

It was a sunny day, early in the school year. James Hill worried about keeping his starter position on the football team. Coach had warned everyone that he'd be taking a close look at their weight-room scores each week, in choosing the starting line-up. Some of his buddies lived right there in town, and could walk to the weight-room. He had to talk his parents into driving him.

Through the open window of the pickup, he heard the tires squeal around the corner a quarter-mile away. When his dad's car started bouncing down the 300-foot gravel driveway towards their rural farmhouse, he frowned, distracted from his own problems. *What's wrong with Dad?*

He killed the engine on the pickup, and by the time the silver Cherokee pulled to a stop beside him in the driveway, James had gotten out.

"Hi, Dad. You home from work early?"

Bob Hill didn't look up for a moment.

Finally, he noticed his son. "You're not at school?

"Teacher work day. Mom's gonna take me to football practice in a minute. Is something wrong?"

His dad got out. "Bring in that cardboard box for me, will you?" He stalked towards the house.

James pulled it out. His spirit sagged.

There was no mystery here. Sticking out of the box was the translucent plastic slab lettered with "Robert Hill" that'd been on the wall next to his office at work for years. Piled like trash in the bottom among file-folders were a dozen little knickknacks he'd seen on his father's desk. James had visited his father's office a couple of times when the company opened the doors for Family Day. He recognized nametags from conferences Dad had attended, several company appreciation awards, even the plastic fish-shaped cozy to keep his drinks cool.

They fired him? How could they fire Dad?

Diana, his mother, was hugging her husband when he brought the box into the kitchen.

Bob straightened. He glanced at James. "I got laid off."

"Oh, Bob. I'm so sorry," Diana said. "I heard on the news that they were letting off another nine hundred workers."

He pulled out a chair and sat down, taking her hand. "It's not like it was a surprise or anything. I haven't done anything useful for the company since Dennert took over the department." His voice was bitter.

James said, "You're not the only one that got laid off, Dad. I know a dozen kids at school who've had the same thing happen in the last few months."

He pointed at all the framed certificates in the cardboard box. "You got all those awards. People are always telling me how smart you are. You'll get a new job soon. I'm sure of it."

James tried to be upbeat. Now was certainly not the time to try to talk his parents into letting him drive himself to school.

"Maybe." His father sounded down, unsure of himself.

Diana said, "Betty said there were openings at Franklin's. I've worked retail before. I should call her."

3

Bob unpacked the cardboard box. He was glad when Diana took James off to practice. His family was a comfort, but he needed to settle his brain. In spite of all the warnings, he hadn't expected it to happen to him.

He thumbed through worn and irregular folders loosely packed in the cardboard box. Most were his personnel records, old copies of presentations given, even a few letters of commendation—from the days before his last boss.

A large brown accordion folder caught his eyes, and Bob's expression grew a little colder. 'Dennert's Damned' that was what he'd begin to call them in his own mind—good ideas, officially ignored. They were totally new project ideas. With a little work and a little funding they could become profitable. The company's official history had made the point that several times, the company had re-invented itself, turning to new businesses as the technology changed.

But times had changed, especially in the mind of his boss. Dennert had tossed them back to him, unopened, unread.

That meeting in his office was burned into Bob's brain. They'd been arguing about the new direction Dennert was taking his department.

"This company has been rooted in innovation." Bob had been trying to be reasonable, persuasive. "We need new ideas, new products, new technologies, to keep us out in front."

Dennert shook his head. "Not any more. We're in a commodity marketplace. The company can't afford innovation. We need to document what we do, and refine that process so we can compete. In our business the profit margins are getting narrower by the quarter. We can't afford to waste our resources."

Bob had come away from that meeting stunned. For fifteen years he had worked for a technology company, where ideas were the fuel that drove it to ever-new markets and ever-new products. The innovator was valued.

Not any more.

Bob's job had been developing contacts in the universities, reading all those scientific papers that often never left the library shelves. That was what he was good at, taking blue-sky theory and seeing commercial possibilities within.

But for nearly a year, under explicit orders from Dennert, and supposedly, the higher-ups who supported him, he was told to toss the new concepts and concentrate on documenting in elaborate detail the step-by-step processes of his job.

Two hundred pages of details, contact numbers, and methods—all of them obsolete the day I wrote them. I'd bet money no one will ever read it. He hadn't bothered to make a copy for himself.

It's my job to provide for this family. But I'm worthless now.

Diana had taken it well, anxious to get a job for herself. *She's mentioned this before. Maybe with James nearly grown, she needs to get a job. It'd certainly help until I can find a new place.*

It just hurt.

He sighed, and plucked the accordion folder out of the junk and slipped off the band.

Half a dozen finely crafted proposals stared at him. With his track record, at least one could be forged into a multi-million dollar business, given starting capital and a dedicated crew.

Of course, all of the others were just money sinks, traps for the unwary. No one could tell the difference without making the effort.

I'd love to turn one of these into a success. I'd love to show them what one good innovation is worth!

4

"Mom?" James asked as they pulled into the mud and grass parking lot next to the football field. "Are you really planning to get a job?"

Diana Hill tilted her head, as if considering the idea. "It's probably a good idea. Your father needs some time to find the right job, and our savings won't last forever. It's not like I have no experience. I worked right up until I went into labor with you. Of course, the school would be happy to keep me selling T-shirts and hot-dogs at the games like I have since you started football, but that's just volunteer work.

"I just think it would probably be better to get paid for my labor, for a while, don't you?"

James hadn't given much thought to the problem of where the money came from. Right up until the moment Dad came home without a job, he had been planning to push the idea that they needed another car, preferably a Jeep Wrangler with a good stereo, raised suspension, and huge balloon tires. There were three drivers in the family. They needed three cars. Something like that would be perfect to take mudding—and to drive himself to school, too.

I need wheels. I'm too old to have Mom drive me everywhere.

He ducked out of the pickup and headed for the locker room. He was suiting up when it occurred to him.

If Mom works, she won't be able to drive me to school.

That was a perfect reason to get a car, but it was the absolute worst time to bring it up. He'd have to think about this some more.

5

James set the box on top of the stack a few days later. He wiped the sweat out of his eyes. The garage door was wide open while they moved the family junk out of the storage shed, but it wasn't air-conditioned and even in the fall, Central Texas could boast some hot days.

His father was right behind him, carrying a large canvas tent over his shoulder. They hadn't used it in years.

"Dad, it's four o'clock."

Bob looked puzzled for a second after he stashed the tent on the growing pile. "Oh. Yes. Your weight room. Can it wait a little longer? I need to get the storage shed emptied out while there's still daylight."

Mom had been working for a week now at the department store, and her hours were getting long. It was falling on Dad to ferry him around.

"I could drive myself."

Bob Hill frowned. "Diana doesn't like that."

James nodded, "I know. I've heard it all. But this isn't a joy ride. I do the driving when Mom takes me anyway. If Billy Timmons hadn't wrapped himself around the light post right in front of her, I would've been driving myself for a year now."

He caught himself before he went into the unfairness of it all. That would hardly impress Dad. Logic worked with his father, not griping.

"Anyway, I've got to get to the weight room before it closes and do my leg presses, or Coach won't let me start next week. If you take me, that's there and back, twice. Let me drive myself and save yourself the time."

His father glanced at his wristwatch. Since the day he announced to his family that he was going to set up a home office and start his own consulting business, Dad had been working long hours every day.

"Okay, but no side trips. I don't have time to calm her down if you're late."

James nodded, "Thanks Dad." He went straight for the pickup, trying to keep a lid on his glee. Dad expected him to be responsible. He'd let it all out on the road, once he was out of earshot.

6

"Hello, James." Her voice was melodic.

"Hi, Suzie." Dripping from sweat after his workout, he was surprised to see her poking her head into the passenger side window of his pickup. Blond and doing full justice to her orange and white cheerleader outfit, she was the last person he expected. He was embarrassed for his sweat, and the empty plastic bottle trash in the floor.

"I like your new pickup." She looked it over, not seeing the wear, obviously.

"Hardly new. I've inherited it now that Mom's gone to work." That was still wishful thinking, he knew. He had driven himself to school five times now, and each was a separate plea. Mom still didn't like it, and Dad kept giving him approval 'this time'.

The past two weeks had been interesting. The storage shed had gradually become Dad's office. James helped clean it up and together they'd buried a phone line and a power cable, just a glorified extension cord, from the house. With a space heater, a fluorescent light fixture and a desk, Dad had a new office.

He grinned, "Finally! I have an excuse to use my driver's license."

"Wheels are wheels." She glanced around at the interior speculatively.

James patted the old bench seat affectionately. "Yeah. I love being the one to give rides to my buddies. My time at last." Squeezing into the back seat of Frank's car with too many guys was fun, but it had been a bit tight.

He hadn't explained to his parents that he'd been driving his friends, not yet, but he intended to. Mom was still too worried about him—still too afraid he would kill himself in an accident.

Suzie smiled at him. "Do you think I could get a ride from time to time? Maybe after practice or after the game?"

"Sure! No problem."

Just then, Drake and Slick came out of the gym and gave him a wave.

Suzie tapped the windowsill. "I'll take you up on that, then. See you tomorrow?"

He nodded dumbly as she sauntered away.

What was that all about?

Guys asked for rides all the time. But girls rode with girls. Unless they were more than classmates.

Suzie Shannon was a junior, like him, and they had shared more classes over the years than he could count, but she'd never paid him much attention.

Girls aren't interested in me. Football took too much of his time, and he suspected they knew that. That and homework kept him busy. Academic suspension was always just close enough to make him nervous.

Slick and Drake dumped their bags into the pickup bed and piled in.

"Hey James, what's up with Suzie?" asked Slick.

He shrugged, starting the engine. "Just looking at my pickup."

Drake rolled his eyes, patting the bench seat. "She's checking out the upholstery."

Slick elbowed him in the ribs. "Be nice, Drake."

James felt hot. He turned the air-conditioner on high.

"Want to hit Wag-A-Bag on the way home? I could use a Gatorade." James asked, to an assenting chorus. The only convenience store in town was a regular stop off on the way home. Drake didn't bother him—he'd had a dirty mind since sixth grade.

Still, James felt energized, tingling all over.

7

Bob Hill, dressed in suit and tie, looking every bit an independent consultant, frowned at the airport shuttle. He was parked out in the cheap part of the lot. *Fiberglass. Just fiberglass.* Lightning flashed, and the thunder was only three seconds later, less than a mile.

A fiberglass hull is no shield at all. They need to put a metal mesh in the mix. The conductive metal box of a car had always comforted him—no one was hurt by a lightning strike inside a Faraday cage. The electricity passed around the box and never went inside.

The shuttle pulled up to the parking lot station labeled G13 and he had to make a dash for his car, his briefcase over his head. At least it kept the driving rain out of his eyes. By the time he fumbled with the keys and started the engine, he was shivering and totally soaked.

No wonder the pilot said we would be making good time—he was trying to beat this storm front.

Bob's preferred route home from the airport skirted around the city. It bypassed the heavy in-town traffic for a two-lane farm road that was lightly traveled.

In the downpour, Bob couldn't see a single other vehicle.

I can't see the road either.

He plowed though a low section where water was flowing several inches deep over the road.

Just keep moving. It'll clear out in a little bit.

He glanced at his briefcase, still covered in beads of water.

Freelance consulting felt like walking through syrup. With Diana's paycheck and their savings, working for himself had seemed like a good idea. He'd printed some business cards and started calling and emailing his wide collection of contacts.

"Hi, Joe. Bob Hill here. I've started an independent consulting practice. Know any good leads?"

At first, it seemed like he had his pick of assignments, but meetings and the overhead of running a small business were killing him.

And he wasn't doing well. This last assignment required a day trip to Dallas to deliver his report in person. He wasn't proud of the work.

In his last job, he'd dug through scientific papers, looking for commercial gold.

Often, scientists working at universities were tightly focused on expanding or disproving a theory. A researcher could be overjoyed at his success in adding a copper atom to a molecule which didn't even have a common name, just a string of symbols. Proving that his theory was correct gave the researcher a better reputation and a better chance of getting funding for his next project.

It took someone like Bob Hill to notice that his process could make computer chips run faster.

When he had taken this job for Terrain Resources, they wanted him to find new land resources—how to make money from land. They already knew about farming, housing, mining, and even newer things like wind turbine farms, so he had ended up searching mountains of papers and reports, looking for opportunities the original researchers had missed. But he was doing the same thing they did. He had to struggle to out think the experts in their own field.

Something has to change. Consulting wasn't making enough money to maintain his family.

I may have to go back to work. There were three corporations near this very road that might take him on—once he'd proven to himself that he was a failure at doing it alone.

His mind drifted back to his orphaned idea folder. There was one that kept bothering his mind. The original author, Dr. Lam Bellerman, had proposed a novel mathematical background for plasma confinement.

It was quite a stretch, rethinking the math into something that could actually be built. But in Bob's proposal, he outlined how such a plasma bottle might be created. If it could, the confinement pressure would no longer be supplied by intense magnetic fields, but by the strange space limits that came out of Bellerman's math.

It would be a fantastically valuable invention, if it could ever be created. His old company might just have been able to pull it off. High intensity fields were needed to start the Bellerman space folding, to create that strange sphere of different space where the intensely hot plasma could be contained. It wasn't something a lone experimenter could come up with in his garage.

If I could just find a flaw in the math, then I could forget about it, and go on to something more productive.

The road approached the river, and began winding. The downpour dropped his visibility down to five or six feet and he had to slow to a crawl to keep his tires from skidding.

I just hope no one is coming up behind me.

Flash-Crack! Lightning struck a power pole just twenty feet off to the side. The whole landscape went green as a transformer exploded and vaporized the copper wire inside. Bob skidded to a halt, his right tires off the shoulder.

He blinked, trying to clear his eyesight from the flash image.

What is that?

Green sparks and ... other things were in the air—the only things close enough to be seen in the downpour.

A glowing ball came drifting down, directly towards him. The size of a toy balloon or a cantaloupe, it bounced weightlessly off the hood of his car. Three seconds seemed like an hour. It drifted inches above the metal, right before his eyes. Then it exploded with a loud *pop!*

Ball lightning. He'd never expected to actually see it in person. There'd been thousands of reports, and dozens of theories. None had proved out. No one had figured out how the plasma of the lightning could be bound up into an enclosed sphere with no external forces.

The parallels to his own musings were startling.

Could ball lightning be Bellerman space?

A car swooshed beside him, horn blaring out its driver's surprise.

Bob glanced at the rear mirror and pulled back onto the road. He drove slowly, but his mind was elsewhere.

8

Cheerleaders in orange and white were clustered around Sam Frederick's new red convertible as James finished practice and walked across the parking lot towards his pickup. Suzie was with them.

He nodded, and Suzie trotted over to join him.

"Hi James." She moved close enough put to her hand on his chest. "Can I have a ride after the game Friday? I'd love to go with you."

"Uh, sure. Do you need a ride now?"

"Oh, no." She looked towards the rest of the cheerleaders. "The squad still has another hour yet."

"I can wait." It would be a stretch. His parents were now letting him drive routinely. Maybe they wouldn't notice the delay. Dad was hard at work in his office, day and night. Mom worked until closing. Still, he hadn't officially told them he was carrying his friends home.

She smiled. "It's okay. I have another ride."

James watched her return to her group. He sighed and then headed home. It'd been a week since she first asked him, and not much had come of it. Last Wednesday, she'd declined a ride at the last minute when she realized she'd have to squeeze in on the bench seat with three guys.

It was frustrating. Slick had even asked for a ride today, and James had turned him down just on the suspicion Suzie would ask.

The girl was too much on his mind. He never listened to gossip before, but now anything about Suzie caught his attention. She'd been Sam's girlfriend until a couple of weeks ago. He hadn't known that.

When he pulled into the driveway, he noticed the garage door open and his father digging into the stacks of old storage boxes.

"What's up?" he asked.

"Hunting for the old forth-of-July fireworks we never got around to shooting. Do you know where they are?"

They hunted together and found them.

"What do you want them for?"

Bob pulled out a larger rocket, with a long stick glued to its side. "Just some research. I read that there was a group down in Florida that fired rockets trailing wire into thunderstorms to trigger lightning strikes. I thought I'd give it a try."

"Cool. Can I help?" Off in the distance, he could see a line of clouds approaching.

"Sure. Let's get up to the fence line. If it works, I don't want to be anywhere near the house."

Bob send James into the house to find one of the clicker fire starters they used to start the gas grill. By the time he got up to the fence, his father had secured some fine wire to the end of the stick, and was unwinding several feet from the tiny plastic spool.

They stuck the rocket into a three-liter soda bottle and waited until the clouds got closer. James claimed the honors.

"Now when you light it, run towards the house. Don't stay anywhere near the fence."

James nodded, a grin on his face. Dad came up with the coolest things. When was it—last year? They'd videotaped a science project showing that gunpowder burning by itself in the air just burned, but if you confined it—they had used a plastic film canister taped shut—it exploded.

Oh, Dad gave him the safety lectures, and warned him about the fatal dangers of pipe bombs, but his Dad had done so many cool things when he had been a kid, and he wasn't afraid to teach him.

The clicker sparked a couple of times before the butane flame lit. He poked it at the fuse, and when it sparked he backed off.

"Get farther back!" his father ordered.

He stepped back another few paces.

Just then, the rocket ignited and slowly climbed, dragging the spool of wire off the ground and arching into the wind.

"Well, that was pathetic," Dad said. "The wire tangled. It barely got a dozen feet high."

"Let's do another one!"

They collected the spent rocket and looked at the tangle of wire and the melted plastic spool.

Bob Hill shook his head. "No, that was the only thirty gauge wire I had. The rocket was too small and obviously I don't know how to let it unspool the wire. I'll have to think about it before next time. And I'll need a more powerful rocket."

9

The house looked deserted when James came home a few days later. Dad spent most of his time out in his office. Some of the days, he drove Mom to work, so that he could have the car, but whatever he was doing on the computers seemed to be taking up all of his time.

After rummaging through the pantry and coming up with a bag of microwave popcorn, he prepared for a snack. Right before he pressed the start button, the phone rang.

"Hello?" "Hello?" Dad on his extension had answered at the same time.

"Hey, Jimbo!" It was Drake.

"I've got it Dad." There was a click.

"What's up?" he asked.

"I left my Government notebook in your pickup. I need it."

James felt a twist in the pit of his stomach. How could he get it to Drake's house? He certainly couldn't come over here to get it. But Dad was home.

"Are you sure?"

"Yeah. I forgot it. So sue me. Can you bring it over?"

"Um. Let me go hunt for it. I'll call you back."

James went out the front door and around to the driveway. He was head down, digging under the seat when he heard the garage door opening up.

He looked up, the worn and dog-eared spiral notebook in his grasp. Dad was standing beside the pickup, garage door opener in one hand, and a tool kit in the other. The movement caught his father's attention.

"James! I didn't see you there." He set the tools on a shelf and pressed the opener again. As the door rumbled he looked at the notebook.

"What have you got there?"

James was tongue-tied for two heartbeats—not a long time at the rate his heart was pounding.

"Uh." He had to say something. "It's Drake's notebook. I need to get it over to him."

His father said nothing for an age. The garage door closed, finally, and he put the opener in his pocket. He glanced at his watch.

"Okay. We promised your mother that you would stay out of evening rush-hour traffic. I'll ride along." And before James could react, he opened the passenger side door and strapped himself in.

There was no choice. James started the engine. His heartbeat sounded louder. Did Dad know he had been driving Drake home? No side-trips. Mom said that. Dad had agreed.

Keeping his eyes on the road, but trying to sneak looks at his father's face as they drove over to Drake's place, James worried about what he was thinking.

When he pulled into Drake's driveway, he killed the engine and reached for the notebook, but his friend was too quick for him. He ran up to the window.

"Hi, Mr. Hill." He grabbed the notebook. "Thanks Jimbo. Sorry for the extra trip. Slick had talked my ear off and I was too anxious to get out of range. Remind me next time, won't you."

James just nodded. His father smiled and returned the goodbye.

When they were halfway home, he couldn't take it any more. "Dad?"

"Yes, James?"

"I've been taking the guys home after school. I know Mom had said no side trips, but it was just impossible to say no."

There was no reply for a quarter mile, but as they approached home, he said, "James, I don't believe it's ever impossible to say no. But I do understand.

"I'm disappointed. I've always wanted you to be responsible. We gave you our trust, and it hurts to find out that you have betrayed it."

James felt his insides twist up. For as long as he could remember, nothing hurt worse than his father's calm disappointment. He pulled into the driveway and turned off the engine.

Dad put his hand on his shoulder. "Honesty is important too. I'm glad you told me. I'll talk to your mother. She's getting used to the idea that you are driving. Perhaps it makes sense for you to help out your friends."

10

Back in his office, the shed's window open to let in a little breeze, Bob Hill sat down at his desk and stared at the stack of bills.

I'm the biggest fraud. How could he come down on his son for hiding a minor infraction from him when he was hiding so much more from Diana?

He hadn't been paying any attention to his family, had he? If James hadn't confessed, he would have been oblivious to it all. With Drake's notebook right there and the boy blurting out what had happened, he'd been lost in his own problems, thinking about the Bellerman equations.

He looked at the bills. Their household debt was climbing, and that didn't even count the three new computers he'd purchased to add computing horsepower to his little network.

And hidden somewhere in the stack of papers was the little check he'd received from his last job. It would hardly cover his expenses. As a businessman, he was a failure. He should confess it all to Diana, and spend his time and energy hunting for a real job.

But the Bellerman space—it was such an intriguing concept. He reached into his desk drawer and pulled out a sketch. The crude diagram for an initiator was the key. If he could just build it!

11

Drake tapped him on the shoulder. "Hey, any second thoughts about the movie?" He set his lunch tray down beside his.

James shook his head. "Sorry. But it's all your fault for forgetting your notebook. Just be happy I've got permission to drop you off after school. Otherwise you'd be back in Frank's car."

Drake nodded across the room to where Suzie was eating with her friends. "I'd bet you'd take her to the movies."

James concentrated on his pizza slice. "Um." It wasn't a topic he cared to discuss.

12

Bob hesitated over the letter he'd pulled from the mailbox.

It's ridiculous to turn down a job offer. His work for Terrain Resources must have made a better impression than he'd thought. Now they wanted a bid for another project. He returned to the shed.

The web browser showed a line of thunderstorms approaching. He let the letter drop to his desk.

I can't think about that now.

An old beat-up folding table in his work shed held two gadgets he intended to connect today.

Unpainted, and missing the fancy decals, was the most powerful model rocket he could find in the local hobby stores. At its base was a trio of H-class engines, much more powerful than the D's he used years ago when he built hobby rockets for fun.

The other gadget was copper tubing in a wooden frame to channel the lightning strike, pinching it into an intense magnetic field. The electronics box was enclosed in a soldered copper shell.

It's the best I can do on my budget. It had taken close to two thousand dollars, and he had no idea what he would tell Diana if she ever found out.

There was a brief rattle of hail on the metal roof of the work shed. *It's coming.*

He pulled on a green poncho and carefully loaded the gear into a wheelbarrow.

As he headed out into the pelting rain, he thought, *I feel like Ben Franklin.*

13

The rain felt good on his head. James grabbed for a water bottle with the rest of the defensive team and labored to catch his breath. Slick was out on the field, trying to crack the Bulldog's defense.

He wished him luck. A dozen times already, the announcer had said, "Play stopped by 53, James Hill". He was doing well, and his teammates had slugged him plenty to show their appreciation.

The crowd came into focus. Normally he tuned them out, concentrating on the game, but today he scanned the crowd.

With his mother at work most nights, he missed her clear voice shouting "Go James!" And his father was out of town a lot doing his consulting thing. He should be here tonight, but he was rarely in the stands. The men of his town tended to walk the fence line, keeping close to the action, shouting encouragement and advice to the players.

Suzie, flushed and waving her pom-poms, blew him a kiss.

The whistle blew, and his focus snapped back to the field.

Everything was football from then on. It was a tough game, but at the end, 21-20 was a win no less. He looked around for his father after the team circled for the coach's last words and the crowd started drifting out onto the field, but with no luck. Then the team went to their bus, the band went to theirs, and the cheerleaders went to their minivan. The drive back to the school was a pleasant celebration, but they were all tired.

After the showers and the congratulations, he went outside. The rain was letting up and many people were standing outside anyway, talking about the game.

Suzie dashed out of a doorway and hopped into the pickup beside him.

"Change of plans," she said hurriedly. "Cheerleaders are having a late meeting, and I've got to stay."

"I'll wait."

"No need. We're going to Julie's house after."

And before he could complain, she leaned into a kiss. His arm went around her and he could have stayed that way forever, feeling the heat between them.

She broke the kiss and left. "Gotta go!"

This is nuts. He sat still for a moment, tasting her makeup and letting his heartbeat settle.

I should ask her out—a regular date. This hit and run stuff is going nowhere.

14

The tires on the gravel outside caught Bob's attention.

The game. I missed his game.

He flipped a switch, and then headed into the house.

James was at the refrigerator.

"Hi. How did the game go?"

His son came up with an apple, and bit into it with a crunch. "Pretty good." He chewed.

"Sorry I missed it. Work stuff got to me and I missed the time."

"'Sokay. Coach told me my goal-line stand saved the game. I believe him. 21-20."

"Oh, you're just trying to make me feel bad."

James grinned at him. "No, really, Dad. It's okay."

But he then proceeded to tell him the whole game, play by play. Bob listened. He missed the games. When he wasn't out of town, he was deeply caught up with his new project.

A little later, Diana arrived. "How did your game go?" she asked.

"Pretty good." And James was off, re-telling the game from the beginning.

Bob got a coke and slipped back out to his workshop.

He paused at the door, his hand on the light switch.

I can still see it. The glow of the trapped ball lightning was fading, but the size hadn't varied. It really was Bellerman space, otherwise his stabilizer would never have worked.

He flipped on the light switch, and the faint glow was lost in the glare of the fluorescent tubes hung by hooks and chains to the wooden rafters of the work shed.

Before James had arrived, he had been tracing the power supply circuitry node by node with his multimeter. The ball wasn't exactly stable. There was a flutter in the boundary of the sphere.

It was three AM when he solved it. Replacing a weak capacitor in the circuit, while it was still running, was exacting work. One glitch and the sphere would be gone, until the next thunderstorm rumbled through.

Resting against the wall was the melted and charred framework of copper that had channeled the power of the lightning strike. He winced at the sight. *I don't want to have to build another one.*

How lucky had he been to create a Bellerman sphere on the first try? He looked back at the table.

Voltage fluctuation had originally caused a disturbance on the surface, like a heat haze that refracted the light just a bit. With his custom-made, battery backed up power supply now rock stable, the ball of folded space was no longer visible.

Now what can I do with it?

Dawn came, and the caffeine began to wear off. He tapped the keys on his computer, listing a summary of the results. The details remained in his notebook. He was too tired to list them all.

"Item 15: I can control the size and amazingly the location of the sphere. I don't understand it. Not at all. When I wake up, I'm going back over the math. How can I have a gadget that controls the actions of a sphere two meters away?"

He shook his head, dialed the sphere down to marble size and went to bed.

15

"Mom? Do you have an employee discount at your store?"

She looked up from her breakfast cereal. "A little one, why?"

James shrugged. "Oh, I was just thinking about getting some new clothes."

Her eyebrows lifted, "Got a girlfriend?"

"No." He frowned. "It's just that all my clothes are old and grubby."

She thought a minute. "Well, Christmas is six weeks away. Wait until then."

"Maybe I can get a job?"

"I've got a job for you. We need to cut out all the wild grapevines growing in the trees near the pond."

"Do I get money for this?"

Diana shook her head. "We don't have any. Times are tight since your father lost his job. The consulting pays erratically, and not very much.

"How are your grades coming?"

James shifted in his chair. "Uh. So-so. Why?"

"Coach Echart mentioned something. He's worried you might lose your eligibility. Adding a job to your schedule might mean that you have to give up football."

"I can't give up football!" He knew his grades were getting bad. The other classes were so boring.

"Then concentrate on your homework. I know you're smart enough. You just need to take the time to study.

"Your father is working very hard lately, and we'll make it past this, but we all have to be patient and watch what we spend."

16

1:47 AM—Bob sighed. *My sleep schedule is wrecked. How many days have I been at this?*

He moved the mouse and clicked open the log and began typing.

"Major breakthrough. Following the math
has paid off."

So many of the elements of the equations were paired, with a right-hand and left-hand symmetry. It'd been a basic element of the original paper.

"Today, I managed to shift the sphere to dual
control elements. Tolerances were very tight and
I think that without computer control of the
circuitry, any further refinement will be
impossible to control."

His mind drifted off into the design of the computer system he would need.

The work shed could get crowded.

It's already crowded.

The shed had been designed as a portable storage building, not a place to live and work. Its wiring was extension cords. Its walls and ceiling were un-insulated sheet metal and wooden framing. Luckily, Central Texas was not very cold, or the little space heater he'd added to the mix wouldn't be enough.

Me, the desk, the heater, the computers, and now this.

The one-foot diameter sphere was visible now, because it was in two places at once.

Forcing the symmetrical elements of the Bellerman space into two different locations did just that. It had twinned right before his eyes.

It is really just one sphere. There is only one inside. It's just that it has two outsides.

Light entering one of them came out both. Looking through them gave a double-image.

He took a pencil from his pocket and tossed it through the left sphere. It exited out of the right one.

Teleportation.

He dropped a quarter through it, and it came out the same side. A penny did the same, but a second penny teleported.

It's random.

The door opened with a creak. A dingy white fur ball of a dog stuck his nose in, sampling the warm air.

"Come on in, Willis. Want to make some history?"

Carefully, Bob dialed up the size of the spheres. *Size is an attribute of the Bellerman space. They will always match.* He shook his head. *Don't think that way. It's just one sphere. One sphere. Remember that.*

He adjusted the positions of the spheres one at a time, lowering them to almost ground level.

"Here boy." Willis suffered being picked up and when he dropped him into the nearest sphere, he sniffed tolerantly at his owner's antics.

Bob looked at the two dogs, calmly waiting for whatever came next, and apparently not too disturbed to see two humans waving at him.

"Come on Willis, come to me." The dog stepped forward and put his nose and head through the sphere, and then his eyes glazed, and he whimpered. From the other sphere there was a splatter and bright red blood spurted across the floor.

Panicked, Bob grabbed at the dog's head and pulled him out. Willis collapsed on the floor. His chest heaved for a couple of times before it stopped.

He's dead.

Blood was still pooling on the floor. He could smell it.

Bob picked up the warm, limp dog, aching to think of anything that he could do. There was nothing.

Teleportation worked, but it was random all the way down to the molecular level. Skin, muscle and bone were all connected. Once Willis poked the tip of his nose out one sphere, the chemical bonds of his body kept all of his body connected. But blood found an easier path out. Powered by a pumping heart, most of his blood was gone in seconds out the other sphere. The dog couldn't survive.

17

Diana asked over breakfast. "Bob, have you seen Willis? He didn't come when I called this morning."

He sighed. "I'd meant to tell you this later, but he's dead."

"What?" asked James, who'd just come into the kitchen to grab a bite on the way out the door. "What happened to him?"

"All I could tell is that he lost a lot of blood. I'll bury him this morning."

Diana said, "I hope he wasn't shot." They had lost five dogs in the years they had lived in the country. Every one was a loss, but the ones that hurt the most were the dogs that got into trouble chasing livestock and took a bullet. County law was clear and protected the farmer, but something like that put a permanent wall up between neighbors.

"No. I didn't see anything like that. Life in the country is dangerous, especially for little dogs." Bob hated to lie, even if the words were true enough.

But he'd spent the night cleaning up the blood, and agonizing over what he had done. Teleportation had to remain a secret, even to his grave if necessary.

It was just too dangerous.

Willis had given him an immediate reality check.

He'd created a weapon that could effortlessly scythe down whole armies, whole nations. If he lived out his life with only Willis' blood on his hands, he could count himself very lucky.

"I should never have let him out last night," said Diana.

"No, dear. He visited me in the work shed last night. If it's anyone's fault, it's mine."

James checked the clock. "I would like to stay. Could you write me a late note for school?"

Bob nodded, and went to get the shovel. Up in the northeast corner of the property were the graves of the dogs that came home to die. Willis was small. He wouldn't have to dig it very deep.

But as he grasped the handle of the shovel, his eyes started to water. Digging graves was the hardest task of all.

18

Another late fall thunderstorm turned football night into a madhouse. The game was called at halftime because of lightning strikes near the stadium. James was confused over the standings. They'd been ahead at halftime, but would the game count? It just might make a difference in whether the team went to Regionals or not.

Suzie was ready to go when he got out of the showers.

"I am soaked. Can you turn the heater up?" She was shivering.

He dialed it up, revving the engine to try to get it warmed up. She scooted close beside him, and he put his arm around her.

"I hate the rain," she said. James was quiet. He didn't mind, usually. It made the ground slippery, and it was harder to hear the calls, but under the pads and helmet, the rain itself wasn't that bad.

They pulled out of the school parking lot and headed in the direction of her house.

She felt good, next to him.

"Do you want to stop by Wag-A-Bag for a coke?"

"No," she said. And then, she looped her arms around his neck and kissed him.

I wasn't ready for that. He forced himself to focus on the road. The streets were wet and the rain was still coming down in intermittent waves.

On the road out of town, she pointed to the bridge over Brushy creek. Eyes bright, with a mischievous grin, she said, "My folks won't expect me for another couple of hours. Pull over here, why don't you."

She pointed to a nearly hidden dirt track. It wound down the grade until it stopped under the bridge.

James put the pickup in park and killed the headlights. "It's getting warm."

"Yeah," she said, and unbuckled her seat belt. "Take off your coat." She tugged off her sweater.

She is soaked. Her blouse clung to her skin and he could see everything by the dim lights of the instrument panel. She smiled at him, waiting as he pulled his coat off.

She didn't have to wait long.

19

Bob monitored the computer screen, watching the indicator dot blinking its three dimensional path. This was the farthest he'd ever sent one of the spheres.

If this works, I might just have a commercial winner here.

Now that he had converted the system to complete computer control, there were a lot of experiments he could try.

The closest sphere, pebble-sized, was on his desktop inside a contraption slightly smaller than a gallon milk jug. Centered inside a quadrahedron, a pyramid with four sides, radio sensor loops listened for a signal coming from the sphere.

Bob had manually steered the other sphere out into the pickup's car radio hours ago. The digital clock ran all the time, and made just a little bit of radio whine. It wasn't much, but tunneling through the sphere, the sensor antenna loops were just an inch away. It was close enough to pick up that faint signal.

When James drove the pickup off to school, the radio moved, bringing it closer to one of the sensors. At computer speeds, the software moved the remote sphere so that it stayed centered. The sphere stayed locked in position, inside the car radio, no matter where it went.

Bob's software kept track of each twist and turn. On the computer screen, a moving dot gave him a detailed track of where the pickup was going.

This is great. The sphere is tiny and enclosed in a box for safety, and yet I can track anything, anywhere, with no GPS satellites or bulky uplink dishes. It will work regardless of cloud cover or tunnels. And it is cheap.

It was still too dangerous if anyone had a clue how it actually worked. He'd have to find a way to sell the service, and not let the technology get free.

All the real equipment was still there on his desk. *Could that work? Sell the service, but never tell how it's done?*

There were refinements needed, of course. For one thing, he needed to overlay a road map over the tracing dot, but that was just software.

It seems to have stopped. The track that had been building all day showed him clearly where the roads were. James had gone to town, stopped at the convenience store, then off to the school, where the pickup had stayed for hours.

When it had started again, Bob realized with a sinking feeling that he'd missed another of his son's football games. This discovery was murder on his family life.

And the game must've been called early. Thunder was still rumbling outside. It was the rainy season. He hadn't even noticed until now.

Expectantly, he watched the screen. *Why did he stop there?* He used the mouse to twist the image on the screen. There was a dip in elevation. *The bridge? Or has the system glitched?*

He checked the sensors. No, all were picking up the buzz of the clock. The pickup had to be stopped.

I hope he doesn't have car trouble. The pickup was getting old. *Water could have drowned out the ignition?*

He might need to go rescue the boy.

But there is a way I can check.

He snapped the lights off in the work shed and dimmed the computer monitor. He went to the software and deactivated the tracking loop.

Tap. Tap. Tap.

He edged the tiny remote sphere up a few inches. *That should clear the dash.*

Then he raised the local sphere. It drifted out of its enclosing pyramid and hovered above the sensor loops where he could see it.

In the dark, he peered through the tiny hole in space, trying to see if his son was having trouble with the car.

Even before he could see anything, the sounds of heavy breathing leaked through.

A girl's bare back was all he could see, and hands—his boy's hands—were fumbling with the straps of her bra.

20

Bob snapped the sphere down in size until neither sight nor sound was coming through.

What can I do? James is only seventeen. Who's this girl?

He picked up his cell phone and dialed his son. *We bought him a phone for emergencies. This qualifies!*

After four long rings, James answered.

"Yes?" He was breathing hard.

Bob forced himself to sound calm and relaxed. It was hard.

"James. Game called early?"

"Uh, yes. The officials didn't like the lightning."

He could hear a muffled sound in the background. Probably the girl. He tried to ignore it.

"Well, how did the game go?"

"14 to 6. We were ahead. I don't know how they will count the game."

"We can just hope for the best, then. Son, could you do me a favor?"

"What's that?" His voice was rushed, nervous.

"I think we're out of milk. Could you stop by the store on the way home and pick up a gallon? Put it on the gas card."

"Uh, okay."

"Bye now."

Bob reactivated the trace and watched the screen. Every second was torment until the tracer dot started backing up along the track only a minute later.

"That's a horrible trick to play on you boy."

He dashed back into the house to empty out the milk left in the refrigerator.

21

Saturday morning, James called Suzie the first thing, but she didn't answer the phone.

She was steamed. She hadn't argued, much, when he had gone back into town and gotten the milk like he'd been asked. She just sat there, arms folded, not even looking at him, until he'd dropped her off at her house.

He was mad at her too, and his father for interrupting.

It had taken him a long time to settle down and go to sleep.

His dreams, what he could remember of them, had been dark and lush. Like a shock, the feel of her skin came to him.

There was a knock on his bedroom door.

It was Dad.

"Hi, James. I'm sorry we didn't get to talk after you got home last night. How was the game?"

James shrugged. "Wet. Half the crowd was gone before they even called it."

"You did well, I'll bet."

He nodded.

His father, closed the door behind him, and pulled up a chair. He gave a big sigh. "Prepare yourself son. This is the 'birds-and-the-bees' talk."

James felt a flicker of panic.

"Now, before I start, am I correct that you don't have a girlfriend?"

James nodded. *Probably not.*

"Good! I can't imagine how much more embarrassing this would be if you already had a girl.

"I assume school has already filled you in on the mechanics of it all."

James felt himself flush, but at least his dad wasn't staring him in the eyes. During the first part, where his dad talked about condoms and the differences between real world sex and movie sex, he tensed up. He couldn't help it. It was like watching the needle go in while getting a shot.

Only when Dad started talking theory did it get interesting.

"There's instinct and there's training. Sexual attraction and the basic moves are certainly instinct.

"But people act with much more complex motivations than that. If you do something good, you get a good feeling. You eat and your stomach is satisfied. You move away from fire and your skin stops hurting."

"You exercise and you get endorphins," James added.

"Right! It's a complex system where actions are rewarded or punished and those responses get trained into the brain.

"I think, and this is just my opinion, but I think that sexual orgasm may be the strongest training system in the human mind. It is intense. It's a reward to the brain.

"So, it certainly looks like a training signal. But what is being learned?"

"To have more sex?" James started to relax, just a little.

"Maybe. But think about it—that's already an instinct. It doesn't need to be trained into the brain."

James thought about it a bit. In spite of the topic, learning and thinking things through with his dad was one of the things he liked to do best. Since he learned to talk, it seemed, his father would announce 'Pop quiz!' and ask about something off the wall that was interesting or practical.

"Maybe ... maybe sexual technique, or something about the girl?" He thought of Suzie, angry at him with her arms folded tight.

"Possibly. But that's a big load of pleasure for something external.

"My thought is that when the orgasm hits, a person's self image is burned into his brain. Just think about it. If a guy is being a sneak in order to get sex, success will burn that self-concept into him. 'Being a sneak gets me sex.'

"Or if a guy has overwhelmed the girl with his macho bluster, then that'll be his key to more sex. Or the same with the guy who has to pay for sex. Or the guy who has lied to the girl. Or whatever.

"It makes sense to me that biology would tune the human brain for more sex. Environments change. Cultures change, and much faster than instincts can cope with."

James nodded, but he shied away from thinking about what he might have learned last night. *Letting the girl call all the shots.*

"You might learn a lot of bad stuff that way."

His father smiled. "A lot of people do. Biology doesn't care about what harm you do to the people around you, or what harm you do to yourself mentally. All that's important to biology is more sex, which means, statistically, more babies with your genes in them.

"I hope and pray that when your time comes, your self image will be of an honorable man who cares deeply about all the people in his life."

Once Dad left the room, James looked over at the phone. He sighed and shook his head. Maybe it was a mistake to think about sex too much. He felt his mouth twist into a grin that was more grimace than smile.

Maybe that's why some Dads give their sons the talk.

22

The map overlay was working perfectly. Bob flew the remote sphere up US Highway 89, to the junction with Highway 64 and turned west. He glanced at the readout on the screen. The scale had long since shifted from feet/meters to miles/kilometers. 884 miles.

Someday, I'm going to just input the destination and blip!—it'll be there. But he was too nervous to do that yet. He wanted to watch every step, just in case he'd forgotten something.

He could see the Grand Canyon. The sphere was small, and there was a whistle of air coming through it. In or out, he didn't know and he was not going to put his hand anywhere near it to find out!

There! The main viewpoint. He remembered it clearly from their vacation a couple of years ago.

Carefully staying out of sight of the spectators, he moved the sphere below the railing where decades of tourists had tossed coins into ravines impossible to reach. He edged the sphere up next to the cliff and engulfed a coin.

The first penny fell through the opening in space and struck the floor hard, bouncing high enough in the work shed to hit the metal ceiling hard.

Bob jerked away, as if he had been shot at.

Potential energy. He paused. The canyon walls were at about 7000 feet altitude, and he was at 600 feet. Falling that distance, the penny must have picked up a load of energy. *It would be like catching bullets.*

It'd been a bad idea. But this was useful information. He looked over the scene. *Mostly pennies. I could work all day and not make much. I'll need to hock something else.*

He had to have money to show for the job that he was supposedly doing. Raiding the coins had seemed like a good idea, but it was a bust.

A tap of the keyboard brought the remote sphere back home.

The clock on the computer screen ticked away the minutes. *James will be out of football practice soon.*

Bob hated to do it, but he put the remote sphere back into the pickup's clock, and brought the tracking map up on the screen. He still didn't know who the girl was, and when James had denied having a girl friend, he had a bad feeling about her. It was horrible having to spy on your son.

When he gets home, we'll do something together. James is growing up fast. Soon enough he won't have time for me.

Until then, he had some math to go over. Every experiment, the sphere gave him something new to puzzle over.

I'm a physicist, not a mathematician. Bellerman space equations seemed simple at first, and then doubled in complexity every time he tried to nail them down.

23

Practice was over. James was ready to go home.

I'm sure I saw the cheerleaders rehearsing in the gym.

There'd been a few snide comments from some of the younger football players. The cheerleaders had to practice indoors. "So sweet they'd melt in the rain."

The seniors on the team made it clear that real football players never gripe about the weather, nor about practice on Thanksgiving week. With the standings so tight among the teams in their district, every first down counted towards the Regionals, if it came down to a tie.

He didn't know where Suzie was, and he didn't care. Extra hours in the weight room helped keep his mind off of her, too. Suzie was avoiding him, but just being in the same class with her notched up his tension level. Taking out his frustration on the weight bench seemed to help.

He spun his wheels a little on the way out of the parking lot.

Sam sure seemed cheerful today. He frowned. *She was just using me to get him jealous, I'd bet. She went with him, and his fancy red car.*

Probably under the bridge with him right now.

He approached the spot. In spite of the rain, it looked like tire prints headed down the side track. He felt a flush of anger.

37

Not thinking, he turned off the asphalt, and bounced around the bend.

Suddenly, there was a huge splash, and he slammed forward hitting his head on the steering wheel. The shadows had hidden the floodwaters, well over the roadway, just a trap for the unwary.

Water began spilling into the cab. The currents tugged at the vehicle. James didn't move.

24

Bob watched the tracer dot approach the map image of the bridge and then slow.

Oh no. He is going to do it again.

This time, he did nothing. He couldn't do anything. He had told the boy everything he wanted to tell him. *If he's going to get in trouble with that girl, he'll do so, no matter what I try.*

Being a parent was the hardest thing in the world. Especially at those times when you had to step back, close your eyes, and pray that your kid did the right thing.

He looked at the dot again, and frowned. The pickup was moving again, but it wasn't on the road, it was following the river.

The sound of the storm raging around him, and the furious downpour broke into his awareness.

He snapped into action. Like before, he moved the sphere. But this time, the lightning flash illuminated James alone in the cab, his eyes closed and water rising all around. The pickup was in the river. It was floating, cab end up. James was unconscious.

Willis whimpered, as blood splattered on the wooden floor.

No choice!

He opened the sphere wide, and as water poured in, he reached into the sphere, grabbed James by the arm, and yanked him through.

Fast. Don't give him time to bleed to death.

He pulled hard, and the boy slumped lifeless to the floor. There was a huge spark as the water splashed all over the floor and shorted out the electricity. Everything went dark.

25

Bob kept the phone to the 911 operator open, giving her updates on his boy, and his progress on the road.

James looked very pale. But he was still breathing.

He was several miles towards the hospital when he saw the blinking lights ahead of him in the rain, he pounded the horn and flashed his lights. The ambulance turned around and followed him off onto the shoulder.

EMS technicians elbowed him aside, as they climbed in to work on James.

Bob fed the details, keeping out of their way. He didn't think James had inhaled any water, he had been knocked unconscious, but the cab had still been floating when he had hauled his boy out.

No, he didn't know how he had lost so much blood. Perhaps the scalp wound?

He hated to lie, especially now. Soon they were racing towards the hospital emergency room.

Bob could do nothing but pray. He prayed hard.

Software Exploration

26

James was bored stiff, waiting for Coach Echart to return to his office. He could've gone over to the gym and watched the basketball practice, but watching the others play without him was uncomfortable.

Not that Coach's guest chair has ever heard of ergonomics. He stretched his back to get the kinks out.

The stack of schoolwork in his backpack was getting lighter. He flipped through the folders again. Everything was caught up with decent grades, other than French, and that was ... well, like a foreign language to him.

The teachers had been very helpful while he was in the hospital.

But Barlow probably did me no great favor by letting me take a 'C' in French without taking her final. I'm so far behind now it's pathetic.

And now, Coach Barlow was spending more time with her girls' volleyball team than her French class and it looked like his special catch-up sessions were over with.

Well, at least I can see now.

If the doctors would just let it go. *I hate that eye pressure machine.* Somehow, he'd lost fluid from inside his eyes. After the accident, everything was out of focus.

The door opened.

"Hello, James."

"Hi, Coach. Any news?"

He shook his head, "No. I asked, but until your doctors sign off on it, I can't let you on the team."

Hope that had been building over the past few days crashed back to the bottom.

"I feel fine. I really do. My eyesight is perfect. I've been shooting goals in my driveway and I'm good at it."

"I know, James. You were good last year. But if I let you out there on the boards, and anything happened, it would be my job."

"It's just not fair. First football, and now this."

"It's insurance, James. This is a poor school district. We can't afford a lawsuit, and no matter what you promise, we just can't risk it."

"I understand how you feel. But next year will be better."

James nodded and left.

One little accident and his whole high school career was shot.

He went to the pay phone and called home. No answer.

Stuck.

His pickup was rusting in the creek bed and his driver's license was parentally suspended—they didn't trust his health either.

One little dizzy spell, and that was last week. I'm fine now.

When he first came back from the hospital, people were anxious to be there for him. Suzie, and the other cheerleaders too, were happy to care for the injured and to hear his tale. Not that he remembered any of it.

That lasted about a week. Slick, Drake and Larry were still checking on him, but they had practice to take care of. He was just an ex-jock.

27

"No. We can't get you a new car." Diana Hill shook her head.

"The medical bills." She sighed. "The only insurance we had was from work, and I hadn't been there long enough for it to cover most of the hospitalization. We talked about selling the house."

James said, "No." This was the only house he knew.

She smiled, "It's okay. Luckily your father got a better paying consulting job and money is coming in, but at this rate it will still be a long time before we pay it all off.

"And the pickup—all we had was liability coverage. We won't see a penny on that."

James said, "I'm sorry."

She patted his hand. "I'm just glad you came through it in one piece.

"It's tough now. Your father is working seven days a week. Even when I come in from the late shift, he's always working, out in the shed on his computers. He's even talking about more travel. It's wearing him down."

James realized the car was a lost cause. *If I hadn't been so stupid as to get jealous over Suzie, none of this would have happened.*

He offered, "I could get a job. Coach told me basketball was out for now. I've got better grades than ever now, and I've still got free time on my schedule."

"But are you healthy? The doctors said you had lost a lot of blood, and they were worried about your eyes, and your dizzy spells. You shouldn't rush your recovery."

"I am doing fine, now. Not a single symptom for a week."

Just then the back door opened and Bob walked in. Diana was puzzled. He had a strange gleam in his eye and he was carrying something.

He walked up to them, set the bowl down on the table, and declared. "Water balloon fight!"

He grabbed one of the brightly colored balloons from the bowl and tossed it at James. It caught him full on, and the residuals splashed his mother.

James gasped and grabbed a couple of balloons and got off one at each parent.

Diana screamed, "Out! Get these things out of my kitchen!"

James and his father divided up the remainder of the balloons and dashed out onto the back lawn, pelting each other with the balloons.

Diana grabbed up her mop, and started cleaning. *What has gotten into Bob?* She saw James race past the window, glee on his face.

But it was good to see them having fun together.

28

James waved goodbye to Larry and the guys. He'd taken the precaution of asking Larry for a ride home from school early. Without his pickup to help take up the slack, Larry's car was as crowded as it'd been before.

No one was home.

Larry had been raving about his new video game console.

James had bragged on the benefits of PC based games. *Nothing like Larry's box is on my budget any time soon.*

He suspected that Larry had the better argument.

But, with games on his mind, he wandered over to the work shed.

There was no lock on the door, just a hasp for a padlock they never used. He looked inside.

Techno-clutter. As usual, there was his father's workbench with its strange gear, a desk, and computers against the wall.

He frowned. *Where is Sleepy?*

Three identical computers sat against the far wall in a rat's maze of wiring. Only the hand-lettered name stickers proclaimed which was which. There had been five—Grumpy, Doc, Bashful, Sleepy and Sneezy. His computer in his bedroom was named Dopey, even though it wasn't on the same network as his dad's work computers.

There were five, now there are only three.

Shortly after Dad started consulting, and began buying more computers, James smuggled his game software out here when Dad was out of town. These were so much more powerful machines than Dopey. The games screamed.

But it took time to re-install the games, and his father had made it clear that games on work-related machines would be deleted without warning. He didn't even have an Internet connection on any of them but Grumpy, which he switched out of the local area network when he needed to use the web.

"I have no time for games, or viruses," Dad had said.

So James had created a game disk image, a huge file that pretended to be a hard disk. To make sure his father didn't stumble over it, he renamed it and hid it off in one of the system directories. His father's machines had so much disk space that he'd never notice.

He had hidden it on Sleepy.

Where did it go?

Dad could be back any minute. But he quickly scooted the chair over to Doc's keyboard and logged in. He had his father's login memorized and feared the day when he decided to change his password.

He clicked over to the network list. He would check each of the machines. They could have been renamed, and the disk image might still be here.

Over two hundred computers appeared in the list.

Strange! Has Dad changed his Internet rules?

Most of them had obscure names, like hp150-4, but there in the list was Sleepy, and even a Happy.

With flying fingers, he burrowed down into Sleepy's file system, and there it was, the game disk image.

He listened. No sound of any car.

Copying the image over from Sleepy to Doc's hard disk was started, and over, in just under a minute.

That was fast! He double-checked it. Yes, the whole image had indeed been copied.

That's not right. File copies over the Internet, even over cable-modem systems, were not that fast. Maybe Grumpy to Doc, right next to each other, with gigabit ethernet might be that fast, but not over a long distance network.

There were disk access lights on each of the three computers. He listed files from Grumpy, Doc and Bashful. The right lights blinked. Yes, indeed, the computers had not been renamed. He listed a file from Sleepy. It zipped across the screen just as fast, but none of the local computers blinked.

How did Dad get on a fast network?

Up out of the chair, he walked outside, peering carefully for wires. There was the power cable that connected the work shed to the house. And there was the telephone line, but that was all. He looked under the shed, in the crawlspace, but there was nothing. Nor was there a satellite dish. *Are there hundreds of invisible computers here in this little shed?*

Wireless? That was how his father connected to the Internet, using the house's base station. *But wireless isn't fast enough either.*

There was a rumble in the distance. On their property, you could hear cars from a mile away.

He raced back inside and logged off.

By the time his father's car appeared in the driveway, he was standing out on the porch.

Strange how his dad's hair had started to look gray. *When did that happen?*

29

Bob Hill worked with the lights off, carefully steering the tiny sphere from table to table in the casino. At each table, he located the box where the dealer kept the house's winnings and carefully removed a chip or two.

This is theft. He jotted down each withdrawal on a notepad, in a column under 'Luxor' and the date. Someday, he would have to find a way to pay it all back.

There was little risk. He took from the stash that had not yet been counted, and took it evenly over many different tables. Maybe the level of theft was so slight that no one would even notice it. And if they did, no one could point a finger at an innocent employee.

When the tally added up to $3000, he put the chips into an envelope and steered the remote sphere to a deposit-box of an off-casino service store. Just like before, they would be converted to cash and electronically credited to a Las Vegas bank account he had opened under the name 'AZ Consulting'.

He closed the sphere and connected to the Internet. Finding that his account had over eight thousand, he used their automated payment service to mail a check home.

Five thousand. That should get us past this week's bills.

Bob blanked the computer screen and disconnected from the Internet. He felt totally drained.

This is wrong. But I'd do it again to pay those hospital bills.

It's just like the state lotteries. I'm taxing the gaming corporations. Certainly my research will be worth it to mankind, eventually?

But there has to be a better way.

He was especially guilty about buying that used Ford pickup from the neighbors. One car was just not enough, not with Diana working and James still needing transportation when his friends couldn't drive him. But buying it with stolen money cost him hours of sleep.

Development of the teleportation spheres was coming along much better, now that he had so much computing power.

But even that was stolen.

No computer system was secure from a person with direct access to the hardware. He had reached into the corporate computer center where he used to work. Rebooting one of the computers after hours, he used one of the standard administrative back doors built in at the factory to gain root access.

Reactivating his old account, he then erased all of his actions from the logs and plugged a network cable through the spheres. The huge computer farm was then his to use.

Hiding as just another employee, he ran his simulations, getting results in hours that he had spent weeks on before. Bellerman space equations were finally coming under his control.

One of the first bonuses was the discovery of a way to clone the spheres. From just a single pair of spheres, he now had the ability to make as many pairs as he needed. From that point on, his computer tap was online permanently.

He sighed and stood up in the darkness. He flipped a switch and the lights came on. All around him were dark stone walls.

I am spending all my time these days in a cave. Still, it's a lot easier to hide my equipment here.

He tapped a command on the computer and a large sphere appeared.

He walked through the sphere and out into his work shed.

He had spent many nights sweating over the equations, plagued with doubts that teleportation would ever be safe enough, practical enough to use. Those doubts were gone now.

47

This is so much better. Teleportation was more than just a peephole for light, now.

Create a clone sphere under certain conditions and its interior space was subject to quantum entanglement. Large-scale objects that went in came out as one piece, not just individual molecules. He could walk through and keep his blood inside his body. When his water balloons had passed through the test sphere without leaking, he had been bursting with excitement. He had been aching to share his joy with someone. Diana still hadn't forgiven him for the water balloon fight in her kitchen.

At a different level, he could entangle sets of spheres, and use the potential energy of one transfer to offset that of another. His new cave was at about 3000 feet elevation, and he could step to 600 feet without fear of smashing to a pulp. Of course, that step also pumped gallons of water from the lower Mississippi River to Lake Dillon in the Rocky Mountains at 9000 feet elevation.

I'll need more water transfers to handle the new energy needs. I have a lot of work to do.

30

"Surprise!" Diana and James chorused.

Bob was shaken out of his thoughts as he walked into the house.

"Happy birthday, Dear."

Oh. I forgot.

Diana had a cake for him, with candles he didn't attempt to count.

"Here, I had planned to give you these on Christmas."

It was a boxed set of James Bond DVDs. He remembered mentioning them once, several months ago.

"Thanks. We'll watch one tonight, okay?"

James presented him with a nice multi-function digital watch. His boy coached him through every setting, and it was obvious that his son had gotten him the very thing he wanted for himself.

With cake and popcorn, they watched 'Dr. No' in the living room. It had been ages since they had watched TV together.

"Didn't they have special effects back then?" asked James.

"The opening logo, with the dancing girls. That's about it." Bob grabbed a handful of popcorn. "It's fascinating. Every movie since then has copied that intro. Show some semi-obscured naked girls dancing and then have James Bond shoot his gun. Minor variations, but all of them have that."

James shook his head. "Not even a car with built in machineguns."

"Was that 'Q' who gave him the new pistol?"

Diana liked the scenery. "We need to go back to Jamaica again. I loved that place."

"You guys were in the Caribbean?"

"Back before your were born," said his mother.

"Back when we could afford it."

They watched it through, and even James was enthralled.

Bob was disturbed.

"It's been years since I saw this last. I didn't remember how evil Dr. No was."

Diana asked, "What do you mean?"

"Well, of course he is an evil genius trying to blackmail the US, but towards the last ... I didn't remember that he turned Ursula Andress over to his henchmen to be raped. And she was, apparently. Did you notice that when Bond rescued her, she was missing her pants?"

Diana nodded. "And James Bond was pretty ruthless towards that girl who betrayed him."

"Yes. I think he's mellowed over the years."

But still, the action flick was fun. James asked to watch the next one, but Bob pled that he was too tired.

Hours later, dreams haunted him. Bob lay in the dark, worrying.

I'm a criminal. I make my living by stealing from people. Is there any difference between Dr. No and me?

Maybe I should just shut it all down—smash the control equipment and go find some honest work.

By 2 AM, he was fully awake, listening to Diana breathe and letting worry gnaw at him. He got up quietly from the bed and tiptoed out to the work shed in his robe and overcoat.

He activated the Internet connection and isolated Grumpy from his secret network.

On the web was a database he had used frequently when he was employed. It listed all the references to a scientific paper. The more the references, the more important the world scientific community considered the paper. He entered Dr. Lam Bellerman's paper.

Four referenced already. He scrolled through the abstracts of the new papers. *And half of them are from other countries.*

One of them was toying with the idea of using Bellerman space as a plasma confinement. *That was my first step.*

That settles it. Other researchers will discover it too. It's just a matter of time.

The question was—how would they use the discovery, once they made that final connection?

31

James got a ride home from school and, as usual, the driveway was empty.

He's gone more often than not, these days.

He checked the work shed.

"Whoa!" Most of the gear was gone. Grumpy was the only computer left.

Is the game disk image gone?

He logged on. *Still a network, but it's different now.*

The dwarves were still there, but most machines were strange. He counted the names—about twenty.

The mystery local network annoyed him. *Where are they?*

The wiring was mostly gone, but there were a number of leftovers. He traced Grumpy's ethernet connection to a strange jack mounted on the floor.

He checked outside again, but there was nothing, no outside wire.

It has to be wireless.

There was a system control for the network, a software control panel. He checked and found there were three network ports; a modem, a gigabit-ethernet, and a wireless card.

But only the ethernet is active. How can that be?

Software can lie to you. He opened the access hatch on the side of the computer.

At school, he had become a student aide in the computer lab, helping with upgrades and network issues. The school had more computers, but it'd always been a secret pride that his family system at home was always just a bit more complex and a bit more sophisticated than anything at school.

With Grumpy's guts exposed, he checked the interface cards. Everything matched.

Dopey has a wireless card. His father had said it was cheaper than stringing cable all through the house.

I can network them together.

His father was always quiet about the jobs he took. When James asked, he'd explained corporate security and how that meant keeping secrets, even from family. That included keeping business and home computers separate.

He won't like me doing this. He looked at the time.

Quickly, he made the system changes to allow this computer to route its network out the wireless card. It was strictly against his dad's rules.

But if I switch Dopey to this computer, I'll be disconnecting from the wireless Internet in the house. So it should be okay.

He logged out, tidied up the changes he made, and left the workshop.

In his bedroom, he logged into the mystery network.

Randomly, he began looking through the program directories. His father had taught him scripting years ago. He could read them.

'Bail'? That's a strange command. He opened it in an editor. It was simple enough.

Access the sphere library and send a string of gibberish to its command function, then delete the sphere library, and then delete 'Bail'? What is this?

And what is the 'sphere library'?

32

"James, how would you like to use my pickup for a few weeks?"

He held out his hand to his father, "Where's the keys?"

"Whoa, not until tomorrow. I've got a new assignment and you've got to take me to the airport."

Diana came into the room. "What new assignment?"

Bob looked at the calendar. "About two weeks, maybe more in Seattle."

"Oh, my. That long?"

"It's necessary. And the pay is twice what I got for the last one. We need the money."

She nodded. But she wasn't pleased.

James asked, "What'll you be doing?"

His father shook his head. "Confidential."

James said, "I'll go call Larry and tell him I won't need a ride Monday."

Oh it will be good to drive again! But I wish Dad could talk about it. There are too many secrets.

By the time he'd chatted with Larry, and admitted that maybe dedicated game boxes were faster, his parents had gone to the kitchen table and begun covering it with bills.

"They will be mailing checks on the first and fifteenth. You'll need to handle the deposits." Dad was giving her the same run-down he had last time.

James retreated to his bedroom.

Dad's going to be busy for a while.

He connected to local area network and took another look at 'Bail'.

I've got to find the sphere library.

It didn't take long. There was an extensive set of scripts that made up the bulk of the library. He pulled up an editor.

That's Dad's code all right, but what a mess. The modules called other modules in the library, by the time he had five editor windows open, trying to trace what the code did, he knew he was out of his league.

Dad has programmed since punch-card days, I'd bet. He calls himself a physicist, but he's always at the computer.

He closed the editors, careful to leave the modules untouched.

'GUI'. That's a stupid name for a program. But maybe it was just temporary. GUI meant graphical user interface.

It's worth a try. He activated it.

A window popped up with buttons and sliders and a control widget that looked a lot like some of his video games. Plain black and white, but it was instantly familiar.

Is that the secret? Is he working for a video game company? There are some in the Seattle area.

He experimented with the controls. 'Create Sphere' was interesting. He tried it, and an options widget appeared.

Options, options, options. He clicked at random; 'Monitor', 'Entangle', and 'Watch'.

"Choose initial location." He scrolled through the list and selected Paris.

Another window appeared, and it showed Paris at night.

Ooh. Great graphics. He could see the Eiffel tower and a blaze of other city lights.

An alert box appeared. "Navigate to Watch." *What does that mean?* He moved the mouse to the navigation controls.

Flying above the city, he marveled at the lifelike images. *Elevation control.* Down went the image to street level, dodging just above the cars. There was even sound coming from the computer's speakers. He could overhear snatches of conversation.

This is just what I need for French class. He never liked the language lab. The stilted actors on the tapes talking through the headphones had never worked for him.

The people of this Paris sounded like real people. He could catch a word or two, but they were all talking too fast.

He wandered through the streets of Paris for several minutes, with nothing much happening.

Am I doing this right? There were no gunshots, no car chases, no narration to tell him what the game play was all about. There was just that command "Navigate to Watch".

What does that mean? It's a puzzle. Maybe nothing happens until I find the 'Watch', whatever that is.

Across the street, there was a store. Smoothly, he moved the view towards it and through the glass window.

There are some watches. Could the GUI mean a real watch, like those? There were over a hundred wrist-watches in the display cases. Choosing one at random, he zoomed close enough to touch. Abruptly, the window closed and another opened.

More 'Options'. He chose a few options at random, and then clicked 'DONE'.

Up popped a little widget, "Name location:". He typed 'ParisWatch'. And 'DONE'.

With not even a sound, all the windows vanished.

Game over I guess. Interesting, but I wouldn't pay to play it.

Still, this was what his father was working on. Maybe it was just one module as part of a more complex and interesting game.

He ran 'GUI' again. This time he avoided the Watch option. When he chose location, ParisWatch had been added to the list. *I should delete that, but how?*

Another location caught his eye—'Home'. *Click.*

The monitor screen appeared. At first it was dark, so he moved up.

There's my house! The scene was too real to be believed. There were the trees, the fence line, and the neighbor's houses. Even the time of night looked perfectly correct.

He looked at the house again. Everything was perfect, down to the satellite tv dish clamped to the chimney. *That is unreal.* He navigated down towards the house. The detail had his heart racing. The pattern of limestone bricks on the wall looked perfect. *This can't be stock images. Was Paris this detailed?*

Abruptly he pulled to a stop. On his computer screen, the window showed the kitchen table where his parents were talking.

"There is another bill from Diagnostic Labs." His mother unfolded the paper. "I think it's the same one they sent us the first month. How long will they wait for payment?" The sound of her voice through the computer speaker was a little tinny.

With nervous fingers James moved the viewpoint down the hall towards his room. He moved through the door like it was vapor. There he sat, peering over the computer monitor.

He looked at the door, but there didn't appear to be anything. He wiggled the controls. The motion caught his eye. There was a ghostly image of a marble-sized ball, in real life, there in the room with him. Slowly, cautiously, he edged it closer. The ball hovered, right in front of his face. It was transparent. He could see the faint shine of a camera lens behind it.

James clicked 'QUIT.' The program vanished from his screen, and instantly the ghostly marble vanished.

He was shaking.

What is Dad up to?

33

James drove his father to the airport. Bob Hill was talkative.

"You need to be patient, and don't overwork yourself. The doctors said that until your blood count is back up to normal all on its own, you can't count on being able to do all the activities you did before."

"I know Dad. But I have a doctor's appointment Tuesday, and I'd bet they find everything perfect."

"Well, let's hope so."

He frowned. "James, I'll be gone longer than before, and your mother will be trying to handle everything on her own. Would you be on the lookout and find ways to help her out? Wash the dishes, do your laundry ... that sort of thing?"

"And when she looks tired after a long day, go talk to her. Sometimes her job irritates her and letting her blow off some steam does her a world of good."

James nodded. "Okay. But you take care of yourself too. We need you."

"I will."

James followed his father's directions and they unloaded at the Terminal level. He took his travel bag and waved James off.

Bob rolled his bag inside and went straight to the men's restroom. Hauling his bag inside a stall with him, he pressed a button on his new wristwatch.

34

James hurried home, pushing past the speed limit by five or ten. His father's flight wasn't due to take off for another hour and he had to keep an eye on him.

Reaching home, he raced up to his room, activated the link and fired up the 'GUI'.

Monitor view. Location: Home. The window opened and he flew it high and fast across the landscape towards the airport. Once inside he kept the view near the ceiling and out of sight. Cautiously, he located the gate where his father's plane was loading. Bob Hill was not in the crowd.

He flew his viewpoint out the glass windows and inside the 737 nosed up to the gate. From a position near the television screen, he peered at each of the passengers as they entered, jostling for position and loading their carry-on luggage.

He's not here.

James kept watch all throughout the rest of the loading. By the time the plane took to the air, he was sure his father had missed the plane.

35

The only way I'm going to find him is to master this software.

Mom wouldn't be home for some time yet. For now, he could be confident he wouldn't be disturbed.

He dismissed the airport window and created another one.

Location: ParisWatch.

The monitor window appeared, solid black.

Is it always nighttime in Paris? He moved the window and it quickly brightened. A pale yellow light bulb lit the old furniture. *I'm in someone's house.* It was a bedroom.

There was a window, and he moved close to it, seeing an evening landscape from the height of about six or seven stories. The other side of the street was filled with stone apartment buildings, all about the same height.

Abruptly, the shades closed before him. Sounds of someone moving come from the speakers on his computer.

He fumbled with the controls and found a way to rotate the viewpoint, slowly.

Somewhere, he was sure, a tiny camera was rotating on a track around a tiny sphere. He remembered the glint of the lens when he brought it to his room.

Someone moved. *A girl.* She was walking out of the bedroom.

Slowly, he tracked the viewpoint towards the door after her. There was a familiar bang. *A glass door.*

A sound of water started. *A shower door.*

He hesitated on the controls, and then moved closer, catching the view of a female form semiobscured behind the frosted glass.

He took a long slow breath.

No. His first instinct was to panic and bail out of the program. His second instinct was to go with it, and move closer. Her slow motions were tantalizing.

How many naked girls could he watch with this thing? Millions? Billions?

But I'm not here to gawk.

He took a deep breath and retraced back to the origin location, the dresser drawer. He moved in, and it was still black inside.

If this thing is a spy camera, then there has to be a way to shine a light in dark places. He pulled down the menu items one by one, and found it. He set the illumination level at low.

There it is. It was the same watch he'd tagged on his first visit to Paris. *Some girl bought it, and took it home.*

That means that the location followed the watch. *How does that work?*

I should've tagged Dad's watch, then I could track him everywhere.

Muffled, he heard the sound of the girl returning to her bedroom. *Time to go.* He closed the display window.

36

My father is a spy. He's working secretly for a government project that's perfected the ability to spy on remote locations using invisible cameras.

He'd seen such things in the movies, but he'd always thought they were impossible.

I need to keep at this. He fired up another window and this time, he chose a Watch option and tagged his own watch.

A new window appeared. "Begin Watch Training. Press a button."

Which button? But there were no hints. He pressed the one on the upper left of his sport watch.

"Name the button:" He typed **ADJUST**.

"Press a button." He did.

"Name the button:" **MODE**.

He repeated the routine for **START** and **LIGHT**.

"Press a button." But he was out of buttons and his watch was a time zone off and blinking in 24-hour mode.

On a guess, he hit the return key on the computer keyboard. He must have guessed correctly.

"Press the activating sequence."

Activating sequence? What's that? The software did not read his thoughts, although by this time he wouldn't have been surprised if it had.

Come to think of it, how did the software know when I pressed the buttons on my watch? It has to be able to sense it somehow.

So ... the watch buttons are an input mechanism to the software. The watch controls the software?

A sense of wonder started bubbling in his stomach.

Okay. Activating Sequence. What buttons to press to start a control?

He'd hate to mess up his watch settings every time he wanted to use the controls. He'd also hate to control something by accident when he wanted to set his watch.

LIGHT LIGHT LIGHT *That ought to do it.*

The computer prompted, "Select Locations." A dual list widget opened. The right hand side had too many entries to count, but he spotted the one he had created. James quickly dragged 'ParisWatch', 'Home', and then 'Base' for good measure to the active list. He clicked 'DONE'.

"Activation Button:" There was a selector widget. He selected **ADJUST**.

Up popped "Actions list."

A car's engine could be heard in the distance.

Mom's coming home.

He was feeling overwhelmed. "One thing at a time," he mumbled, and clicked 'DONE'.

"Name this watch:" He typed 'Homewatch'.

The window closed. *Does this software give you error messages?*

It was his father's software, he was sure of it. Dad was good. Surely he wouldn't just close the window on failure.

But now he could hear tires on gravel. He hurriedly logged off.

Maybe I shouldn't be doing this. Maybe it's for the CIA or something. Every time I add a location, they could notice and get Dad in trouble.

"James? Did you get your father off to the airport okay?"

He headed in her direction. There was a whiff of fried chicken.

"Yes. No problem."

Should I tell her? She's my mother.

But how could he bring it up. *"Oh, Mom, by the way I think Dad's a spy for a super-secret government project."*

The wind-up clock over the fireplace mantle chose that moment to chime the hour.

It's late, and I have homework I haven't touched.

37

A bubble flicked into existence among the deep sand dunes of Algeria. In transparency, Bob Hill stood carrying a large sledgehammer.

He pressed a button on his watch, and a ten-foot gray granite ball appeared, hovering in the air. It was an image out of fantasy, something you could see in a painting, but never in real life.

But Bob had seen it many times now.

It's hot out here.

He waited, as the intense sunlight baked the hard rock.

Crack! The ball fell out of the sky and hit the sand below, with a *Whoom.*

Good. I won't need the sledgehammer. Just bake it in the sun and natural expansion will fracture the boundary.

The ten-footers were too big to handle personally. The size was intimidating. When he first started carving his base out of granite as one-foot, and then three-foot spheres, a tap with the hammer would break them free.

But it wasn't like scooping out the granite with an ice-cream scoop.

He could teleport a ball of granite into mid-air, but it took just a little extra for the rock to let go of its original strata.

With one location of a sphere in rock and the other exposed to bright sunlight and oxygen, the granite eroded. Just a tiny fraction of an inch deep, rock that had never seen air or ultraviolet light oxidized into a weaker form.

But that was all that was needed. Granite that had formed deep under the ground had been compressed since it cooled out of the magma. Now allowed to expand, it broke loose. In a *crack* the rock ball fell through to the open-air side, leaving a spherical hollow in the orignal granite layer.

Bob stepped back from the desert through the teleport portal to his underground base. In the cave, even with the lights on, it was too dark to see well. He was blinded by the desert sunlight. He fumbled over to a handy computer screen and turned up its brightness. A few copy and paste operations, and he'd set up a group transfer.

Near where the first granite ball fell, twenty giant spheres appeared over the Sahara sands. From halfway around the world Bob monitored the four by five array. Some of them were only partial spheres, with sections cut out by previous transfers.

Inside his base, Bob felt a tremor. One of them had let go. The new room he was creating, just a few feet away was instantly a little larger.

One hundred yards by fifty—it will take some time to get this rock gallery carved out. Can I program this? Automation was his first impulse these days.

He set up the initial parameters and turned his computer loose on the job.

38

The table shook, but Bob only touched his fingers to his drink to make sure it wouldn't spill. He'd quickly gotten used to the background noise. The computer code on the screen consumed all his attention.

An alert buzzer sounded. He frowned and checked some readings.

Time to open a breathing hole.

The carved chamber had no access to the outside, but it was large enough that he hadn't yet dealt with the problem of continuous airflow. *It should be better once I get the big gallery connected.*

He opened a temporary portal to a forested meadow in New Zealand and let the sun shine in. Fresh air was nice. He leaned back in his chair and closed his eyes for a moment.

I need to set a sleep schedule and keep to it. All this preparation, all over the world—it's draining me.

He opened his eyes. The sunshine illuminated his base. The inside walls reflected the sunlight as hundreds of tiny suns. It was a polished granite honeycomb, where the balls had been scalloped out.

I'll break through to the new gallery once the dust settles.

"Computer. Transcribe a log entry." He saw the window open. The voice commands were working out nicely. He still liked to keep his hands on the keyboard, but routine things, like keeping his private blog current, were non-critical enough that he could voice operation while his hands were left free for more precise jobs.

"I've completed the Armory survey. The Russian job should be much easier than the French one.

"I also finished my network isolation last night. There's no longer any outside connection, and I find it stressful. Cutting off my last tie to the computer at home was symbolic.

"If I make a mistake, I'll never see home again."

39

James offered to take Drake and Slick home, but they elected to go to Larry's house for some after-school gaming. Larry invited him too.

Sorry, but nothing you have on your game box can compare to what I have on my computer. Not that he could tell anyone that.

He headed straight for his bedroom. The network login failed. He checked the wireless connection. *It's down.*

The work shed looked more deserted each time he visited. He sat down and logged into Grumpy.

Everything's gone! There was nothing in the file system but the operating system. On a hunch, he checked the utility that monitored disk fragmentation. As a system is used, the data tends to get scattered all over the disk.

Clean as it can be. This has to be fresh installation.

That's why the wireless link went down. Dad had wiped the hard disk clean and reinstalled the operating system. His secret wireless link was gone with all the other customizations.

He tried the network. *Nothing at all. No mystery net. No other machines.*

The ethernet cable still went to the connection box, but a screwdriver showed that there was nothing inside the box. It was just a sheared off section of cable.

Dad cut me off. No programs, no sphere library. Did he see what I'd done?

40

Bob pulled the dust mask off his face and climbed off the little bobcat mini-dozer. The gravel crunched beneath his feet, and a half dozen sunbeams illuminated the newly graded floor of the stone gallery.

My own private underground football field.

The roof looked like a massive egg crate, hundreds of spherical cavities arranged with mathematical precision.

He reached for his wristwatch, the one James had given him, and tapped one of the buttons.

A baseball-sized sphere appeared next to his head. A microphone was visible inside.

"Log entry. I've completed the gallery. Everything is ready for the equipment. One thing I noticed in all of those James Bond movies is that the villain always has an elaborate home base. This'll have to do for me. Those villains always had a private army to do the grunt work for them. Unfortunately, I'm a little short on manpower. Who can I trust?"

41

Ring! "Hello. Oh, hi Bob! I've been hoping you would call."

James sighed as he heard his mother talk. It'd been three days since the network link vanished. The fear had been growing that his father would never come back.

He walked up. "Can I talk to him?"

She nodded. "Just a minute," and handed him the phone. "Dad?"

"Hi James. How's school?" He could hear sounds in the background. A bird screeched. *Seagull.*

"Oh like normal, I guess. Where are you?"

"Seattle. I'm down at the docks right now. It's sort of like a little fair. People selling balloons and fresh fish from push carts. You'd like it."

"I wish I could be there."

"Are you okay, son? You don't sound well."

He sighed. "It's okay." He walked the portable phone into the living room. "I just ... I just didn't know if you were mad at me."

There was a pause. "No. I'm not mad at you. Are there any problems I can help you with?"

"No. Not really. I just wish you were home."

"So do I. But James, you are my son, and even if there are problems, nothing can destroy my pride in you. I love you. Anything else we can work out, okay?"

"Yes, I guess so. But really. I'm okay."

"That's good. Problems happen. We make mistakes. We all do. Promise me that if I ever make a big one, you won't stop loving me either."

42

Bob flipped his cell phone shut, and ordered smoked salmon from a street vendor.

James is having trouble with that girl again. What a time to be away from home.

But if everything goes smoothly, I can be home by next week.

He sat on a bench and picked at the hot meat from its wrapper.

No. Don't count on it. Move too hastily, and everything could fall apart. Bond villains always failed because they considered themselves too smart or infallible.

Every plan fails, eventually. I've so much riding on this! I could destroy everything with one wrong action.

The other scientists following up on Bellerman's paper were still hard at work. Every day he opened a spy portal and checked their progress. He was still far out in front of them all, but he was just one man. All that could change overnight. There was also the chance that he'd missed some other group.

Teleportation changes all the rules of society. He could spy on anyone. So could anyone else. Privacy and private property could vanish. Like a crystal forming, a new society would form out of the existing one. One with new rules of behavior. It was up to him that the seed of the new structure would be the right one.

I may have to give my family up entirely, to keep them from getting sucked into this. I've already made that decision. It's too late to back out now.

Announcement

43

"Rudy Ghest, I'd like you to meet Patrick Mullan, from the Lyon office."

"*Bonjour, Monsieur Mullan.*" Rudy held out his hand.

The French Interpol agent smiled and shook it.

"*Enchanté.* You are our new convert from the FBI?"

"Since the first of the month. Mr. Jackson here is still teaching me the ropes. Interpol has a different flavor to it."

"Hopefully you will have a better time of it. The USA is gradually learning that we can be useful."

"Are you here with the President's entourage?"

Patrick shook his head, "No, we have to pay our own way, but having the French President get out of the Elysée Palace and speak at the United Nations General Assembly was a good excuse to hold another conference on international crime here in New York."

Jackson nodded, "That's why we're here. Lots of people to meet, and no additional travel budget to worry about."

Patrick Mullan waved at the seats. "He's about to speak, would you care to sit with us?"

Jackson demurred, "Thanks, but we've got to hurry."

Rudy followed in his footsteps as they exited, down the corridor to the UN security office. Jackson had wrangled an invitation to view the speech from behind the security cameras.

He peered over at the monitors where one held the pre-released version of the speech.

"DISCOURS DE MONSIEUR JACQUES JOSPIN PRÉSIDENT DE LA RÉPUBLIQUE DEVANT l'ASSEMBLÉE GÉNÉRALE DES NATIONS UNIES

"A L'OCCASION DE LA..."

Where is the English version? He knew joining Interpol would require him to work on his languages, and this new president was a stickler for never using English.

Luckily, since he was a US Interpol agent, he would be dealing with Americans, but still, what was the point of international information exchange if he couldn't speak the languages?

The French President approached the microphone to give his address. It had been billed as an important statement on terrorism and all the news media were ready, with a stable of translators.

President Jospin got several paragraphs into his speech. The crowd of dignitaries and news media were listening patiently, some through simultaneous translators.

Then, a bright light appeared behind his head.

The startled noise from the crowd brought Rudy to his feet.

A giant glowing ball moved high above the podium, its brilliance swamping out the stage lights on the President. The speech stuttered to a halt.

"Greetings to the people of the world." The voice was computerized and distorted. It was loud enough to shake the walls. *"Salutations aux personnes du monde."*

Other greetings came, in a dozen languages.

The UN security agents were scrambling. Commands were being shouted into radios. "Track down where that is coming from!"

Rudy assured himself that all the recorders were running, and then ducked out. He had to see this for himself.

The disembodied, stilted voice was saying, "The rest of this statement will be in English."

Thank God for small favors. Rudy edged closer to the podium. The aisles were already crowded with people urgently moving in both directions. The one word that repeatedly drifted from the crowd was 'terrorist'.

"Unknown to you, I have wrested sovereignty from all the nations of the Earth. This day I have become your Emperor."

Oh no. We've got a kook.

"Imperial taxation shall be up to one billion US Dollars equivalent per nation per year. You need not gather nor deliver this tax. Appropriate goods and services will be taken directly. Fair-minded national governments will see that the suppliers are appropriately compensated.

"Your Emperor has the welfare of all humanity at heart and those who acknowledge his control and cooperate with his actions will prosper.

"A token of Imperial sovereignty is taken immediately from the permanent member nations of the Security Council."

A ripple of red fabric appeared to jump out of the stage, so quickly that Rudy couldn't see where it came from. Like a bullfighter's cape, the fabric waved and snapped, and then disappeared just as rapidly.

Five platforms were arranged side by side where there had been nothing. Rudy blinked. *That's the best stage magic I've ever seen.*

Suddenly, President Jospin shouted, and strode over to the closest.

That's the Mona Lisa. I thought it was in the Louvre.

So, apparently did the President. His bodyguards came running, and he had them surround the painting.

Other national delegations were on their feet as well.

Quickly, the UN security forces were forced to play buffer between the clusters of security guards that were collecting on the stage to protect their national treasures.

The voice from above continued.

"All these treasures now belong to me. Remember that."

And then, the glowing globe vanished.

Jackson came up behind him. "I think your introduction to Interpol is over. Here's your new assignment—connect with the FBI. You're our Emperor contact."

44

The television reporter was listing the 'tokens'. "In addition to the Mona Lisa, just reported stolen from the Louvre museum in Paris, the Russian treasure is a Faberge Egg stolen from the Armory Museum in Russia. It commemorated the 300th year of the Romanov Empire. The British Imperial Crown was reported missing from the Tower of London just moments before it reappeared in New York. The robe is reported to be a yellow Dragon Robe worn by the Emperor of China in the Qing Dynasty, missing from the Forbidden City Palace Museum in Beijing. In contrast to these great artworks, the 'token' from the United States appears to be a stack of ten gold bars taken from Fort Knox, Kentucky."

James watched with an open mouth. Behind him Coach Barlow tried to calm down her French Class.

It had been a fiasco for her. She'd spent days arranging for her two classes to meet together to watch the French President's speech, live on CNN—without the subtitles.

And then, it all fell apart when the Emperor spoke.

"James, get back to your seat!"

He blinked. He didn't even realize he had gotten up out of his chair to get closer to the TV.

Is this Dad's work? His heart hammered. He moved back to his chair as if in a daze.

"Initially, reports were that the 'tokens' were copies of the original treasures, but with the reports now coming in, it appears that a simultaneous international theft occurred across the world, just moments before the UN announcement."

CNN was in high-drama news mode, and the French President's speech was forgotten. Coach Barlow realized that finally and went up and turned off the set.

Suppose there's more to the spheres than just invisible spy cameras. Could you move objects through them? That's teleportation!

It would be trivial to raid the world's treasures then, just pluck them through a sphere.

And then leaving them on the stage, that almost cinched the idea that his father was involved. He'd never steal anything for himself, but as a demonstration? Maybe.

He had to find out!

45

Rudy Ghest reviewed the tapes. Reports were coming in from other law enforcement agencies. The 'tokens' were authentic. And the thefts had taken place far too recently to be real. The European treasures had all vanished within a thirty-minute period, about an hour before they had reappeared on the stage. Not even a military jet could have transported them across the ocean that fast. The theory of the moment was that they were stolen earlier, and replaced by holograms or some other duplicate good enough to fool the first class security measures in those national museums. But no one could figure out how the duplicates were able to vanish without a trace.

Rudy stepped through the video frame by frame, paying particular attention to the red drapery. It appeared out of a single point near the podium, and then when it disappeared behind the treasures, he could see it withdrawing back to that same location. While the view had been obscured, the treasures had appeared within a second or two.

Much better than Las Vegas.

He scratched his chin. *Five impossible thefts. A Wizard of Oz-like manifestation in the UN building. No demand for action from the nations of the world, just an announcement of his Empire.*

This Emperor is not finished. The thefts made no sense as thefts.

Okay, the crowns and jewels aren't fenceable. But those gold bars—melt them down and the gold could be sold anywhere.

And why steal impossible items, and then return them immediately.

What if his billion dollars a year, per nation, tax was not just a theatrical flourish?

Had some genius somewhere invented a new way to steal?

46

The new printer printed the ornate, yellow, dollar-sized certificate, sliced it to size, and dropped it into the waiting envelope.

Bob picked it up with tongs and dropped it through the small sphere floating above his desk.

That's done. The sphere vanished.

He got up from his desk and turned to the large crates resting on the gravel floor. In the background, CNN was playing, listing the events of the theft time after time. He listened with half his attention as he took a crowbar to the first crate, revealing a large rack-mounted computer with an impressive array of computer hard disks.

It'll be days before I can get them all on-line.

47

James skipped out of the lunch line and retired to the bathroom. He closed the stall door, just to get some isolation. He struggled to make sense of what had happened.

Did Dad go to work for the Emperor? What if he is the Emperor?

It sounded almost like one of those James Bond movies they'd watched after Dad's birthday. By now, spies from a dozen countries would be getting their orders from obscure agencies to go out and get the Emperor.

He felt a twinge of fear. *I hope it's not Dad.*

If only I had the sphere library back!

He glanced at his watch, remembering the whole watch calibration thing. *What had that been about?*

He pressed the **LIGHT** switch three times. Nothing.

He pressed the **ADJUST** switch.

"Yaa!"

Abruptly, the world twisted around him. He had been standing, now, he was flat on his face, after having fallen a couple of feet. His head was spinning.

What happened?

The breeze was cool. It was early evening.

He struggled to his feet. Streetlights were on and he was at the curb of a street, between a tree and a strange looking car.

Just a few feet up ahead, a young woman was walking away from him. Something about her hair caught his eye.

Is that the girl from the shower? He could see a watch on her arm.

If so, then he was in Paris!

It felt like the world was reeling again. By the time he shook off the vertigo, the girl was now a block away. He stepped out on the sidewalk, following her.

The city was an attack on his senses; everything was so normal, and yet so different. Things his eyes had skipped over on the computer screen were here, in real life, impossible to ignore.

"*INTERDIT SAUF CD-CMD—INTERDIT A TOUS VÉHICULES LES JOURS DE MARCHÉ*" proclaimed a white sign.

The street signs are in French, and I can't read them. The light posts were old-fashioned, even the trees looked different.

The girl stopped and looked down the cross street, and he got a good look at her face. *Beautiful. Like a model. Or maybe all French girls look like that.*

He followed. Other people caught his attention. No, not all French people were beautiful, but even the old men looked thin, like they ate less.

After a couple of blocks, it seemed he had to walk faster to keep up with her. The streets were a maze of unfamiliar names, yet dotted with familiar logos or signs.

Across the street, he saw a Shell Oil station, but it was just a hole-in-the-wall storefront in the middle of the block, with a couple of pumps at the curb in among the trees.

When he looked back for the girl, she was gone.

James trotted ahead, and then paused at the intersection. No sign of her in any direction.

The Eiffel tower was glowing like it was covered in Christmas lights, off in the distance.

He just stood there, beginning to wonder why he was even following her.

I'm in Paris, with no idea how to get back.

Was lunchtime over? His watch was blinking the seconds, waiting for an adjustment. If he touched another button, what would happen next? He tried to remember what he had set as the options, back then.

He had to try something. He looked in all directions down the lanes and then moved between two trees.

All of the locations had been on one button. He remembered that much. He pressed **ADJUST**.

From the shadows of a doorway across the street, the girl watched as the man who had been following her went transparent and then fell into nothingness.

48

"Hello Rudy. How's life in the international set?"

"Hi, Jay. It looks like I'm off to a running start. I just got tagged to investigate the Emperor."

FBI Agent Jay Russo shook his head in sympathy. "I told you not to go."

"Oh, but this way I get to come back and pester you for answers."

"Rudy, it was you who told me Interpol was just a big database. So where's the data?"

"It's gotta come from you guys originally."

"Seriously," Rudy lowered his voice. "The noise up the line is that nobody knows anything. They aren't even sure what to put on the Blue Notice."

"What's a Blue Notice?"

"A request for information—like what the perpetrator's true identity is—things like that. We spread the net wide, and then feed everything into the ICIS database. You get the results after it churns a bit. I'm the guy who gives it to you."

Jay looked at him speculatively. "Me personally, or the FBI?"

Rudy smiled. "Is there a reason you ask?"

"Oh, quit the kidding. You know there's going to be a task force on this and I'm dying to be on it."

"Then go for it. Tell your boss that you've got the best connections with Interpol and you won't be too far off the truth."

"Seriously?"

"Sure. I'm the Interpol point man. I'd rather work with you."

Jay beamed. "Okay, then I go first. Those 'tokens' weren't the only thefts today."

"No?"

"No. Several mysterious high-tech thefts have just happened. And each time the equipment was stolen, an envelope was left with payment, in the form of a yellow ... not a bank note, but something like that. A promise of payment in the name of the Empire of the Earth."

49

James gave out a *whoof*. He was flat on his face in his father's work shed.

He pushed up. *I never knew teleportation gave you bruises.*

On his wrist, his watch made no sense. He looked at the dumbed-down Grumpy, with the little clock digits in the corner.

Five minutes to get back to class. But my car is at school.

He brushed the dust off his jeans.

At least I don't have to scare up a transatlantic plane ticket.

The blinking digits on his wrist tickled his memory.

The first location was the 'ParisWatch'. The second was 'HOME', obviously a location his father had set. There was at least one more, he was sure.

What do I have to lose?

He pressed **ADJUST**.

This time, he stepped forward, and it was like a quick shift of an uneven floor. The curve of the Earth! That was it. Each teleportation gave him a different down direction. If it was mild, he could keep his footing. The distance to and from Paris made a significant shift, and he fell down.

But where was he now? It was black, and there was gravel underfoot. He took a few steps and hit his shin on a bench. He stifled the 'ouch' impulse. Stay quiet.

No time to explore. Was there another location?

ADJUST.

He fell against the outside of the toilet stall, back in the high school bathroom.

"Hey!" came the complaint from inside the stall.

James stumbled out into the hallway. He was back, but not exactly. He'd started inside the stall. Was the software smart enough to move him out of the way if a destination was occupied?

If Dad wrote it, it just might be.

The school bell rang.

He made a dash for his next class. His mind was fuzzy. Jumping time zones had scrambled his sense of time.

But now he knew what his watch could do. Paris, Home, someplace dark, and then back to his origin.

I'm hungry. The perils of skipping lunch. *There had been a sidewalk cafe in Paris. I should have stopped.*

He should have picked up a hamburger, or whatever it was that the Parisians ate.

50

Rudy examined the banknote with gloves and tweezers. Jay watched over his shoulder.

"I was trained by the Bureau, remember. I'm not going to contaminate it."

Jay shrugged. "Orders."

It was an ornate yellow bill, on good paper with a distinctive texture. The amount listed was 100,000 Imperials.

Jay commented, "The amount taken was very close to $100,000 dollars. So he may be paying for what he takes, only in his own money."

"Can we track down which printer made these? It's not cheap work."

The FBI man held out the envelope and retrieved the Imperial note. "We had the same idea, but the goods bought with this note were a model 5800 Hancock printer and a large quantity of its ink and special paper. I have a feeling this was his very first purchase. He has enough stock to print Imperials for a long time, if these are all he makes."

Rudy said, "So, he had the design all ready to go, swipes the printer, prints his cash, and pays for it on the spot. Nice."

Jay nodded. "But if he is gracious enough to document everything he takes, it'll make our job easier. These notes would be hard for a random thief to duplicate. Did you notice the funny long serial number? Every one is different, and no one has come up with an idea what it means. Is he sending a message?"

Rudy had noticed the number. It was twenty-four characters, full alphabet, uppercase, lowercase, and digits. No punctuation. "Or he may just be adding a method to defeat counterfeiters, just like a legitimate nation."

"Why would he do that?"

"Suppose he's telling us the truth, by his way of looking at it. Paying for goods wouldn't count against the billion dollars. That'd just be a line of credit."

"That's bunk."

Rudy nodded. "It is now, but I keep wondering, why did he announce himself to the world in the first place? We haven't a clue how to stop these disappearances, and the only help we're getting is from him. He's playing a deep game and we don't know the rules yet."

51

Bob broke through the surface, and swam with easy strokes toward the shore. Every time his head went under the water, he could hear the faint, crisp chatter of the parrotfish chipping away at the coral.

He drifted to shore and let the surf nudge him as he rested on the sand.

A two-hour vacation is better than nothing. He needed to sleep tonight. Phase one was complete, but now the real job started.

He needed help, but he was also sitting on total riches. Hiring help would be risky. That much money and power was a huge temptation. Let anyone too close, and he risked losing his life, and the safety of the world. He would have to move very cautiously.

A lovely young blond in a sarong and a nametag came up.

"Would you like something from the bar, sir?"

Jeanne. UK. *These places have quite an international staff. That's nice.*

"Yes I would. How about a virgin Piña Colada?"

"Right away, sir." She smiled and headed back to the bar.

Oh rats. I forgot to bring money. He walked into the shade of a nearby palm tree and pressed his wristwatch.

A moment later she returned. He handed her a twenty and nodded her away.

The last time I had one of these was with Diana.

52

Mrs. Hill had the bills spread out over the kitchen table when James came in from school.

"No late shift today?" he asked.

"Well, I had requested an earlier shift, and to my surprise, they agreed. In that place, it doesn't take a lot of time to build up seniority. By three months, I'm established. If I last a year I'll be up for a management position."

He laughed. "Seriously, how is the job?"

"So-so. The work isn't hard. It's the customers that get to me."

"Jerks?"

"Oh, I get some of those. But the ones that wear me out are the ones who think that they can haggle me down on the price. Here in Texas we get a lot of customers from South American countries that come into a shop like that and stock up on linens or other items. Big purchases and it would help on my commission, but I don't have any authority to change the prices. From their culture, that doesn't make any sense. I explain, and they think I am trying to cheat them."

"Can you get a different job?"

"Quit? No. I still need the paycheck and I can tolerate it."

"Is money still tight? I thought Dad was getting more money?"

"We're in better shape. The checks are coming in. But it'll be awhile before we can start thinking about a new car, if that is what you are asking about."

James shook his head. "No, that wasn't what I meant. I was just worried about you."

"That's sweet. Things are okay."

He noticed the phone. "Have you heard from Dad, lately?"

"No, why?"

"Well, the athletic banquet is coming up. I was hoping he'd be able to make it."

"Well, you know the place he works is outside the cell phone coverage area. We can call him, but I hate to fill up his phone's voicemail."

"Could you do it? Please."

She agreed, and made the call. As expected, it immediately went to the voicemail.

"Don't count on it, James. Even if he could get the time, travel is expensive."

53

Greg Archer paused, thumbing through the want ads.

"Salesman Wanted—Mobile personable multi-lingual representative needed for international high-tech service sales. Great potential. Response G-12."

He looked up at the nearly empty car dealership showroom. *I make enough here to pay my rent, but I can't live this way.*

The 'Mobile' appealed to him. If it didn't say that, he would suspect it was just another telemarketing firm. The 'Great potential' he discounted. The potential was up to the salesman. The multi-lingual and high-tech aspects might be a problem, but that could wait for the interview, couldn't it?

He called the paper and accessed the G-12 voice mailbox and made his pitch.

54

Slick came into the lunchroom and scanned the heads, looking for his good buddy James. His eyes lit up and he wound through the crowd of students, plates and last-minute homework assignments, dropping into the seat next to him.

"Hi, Slick."

Slick just stared at him, grinning.

James waited, but Slick wasn't going to budge.

"Okay, what is it?"

Slick glanced around the room. No one appeared to be listening.

"Sam just dumped Suzie."

"What?" James was puzzled.

"Out in the parking lot, just now. I saw it." He shook his head, relishing the memory. "She shrieked like a banshee. I'm surprised you didn't hear it in here."

James tried not to be interested. "What's the deal?"

Slick's grin widened. "Sam came in late last night and got the inquisition from his parents. They hit the roof, and laid down the law. Drop Suzie, or drop the Corvette.

"That Corvette is a really sweet ride." Slick added thoughtfully.

James was disgusted at himself for the slight increase in his heart rate. Suzie didn't care about him. He turned back to his lunch.

Slick nudged his arm. "So? Are you gonna make your play? You've got wheels again."

He shook his head. "Sorry. Not interested."

Slick sighed. "Suzie will be real disappointed then."

James concentrated on his food. He had other things to worry about, and Suzie was a complication he really wanted to avoid.

When Slick couldn't get a satisfactory rise out of him, he headed off to greener pastures and James retreated from the lunchroom.

Suzie was in his math class, last period. James dashed through the halls between classes and struck up a conversation with Coach Avery about spheres and how to calculate the rates of volume and surface areas. He managed to keep it running until the Coach had to call his class to attention. Suzie tried to catch his attention, but he was very deeply interested in his books all through the class.

James looked at his watch, but it was just habit. It was set wrong and he dared not correct it. Maybe the teleportation functions timed out, but maybe they didn't.

The wall clock crept towards the end of class. James caught the teacher's attention, and nodded towards the door. *Can I leave early?*

Avery had been the football defensive coach, and James always had been one of his favorites. One of the best things about being on the team was that, in this school, jocks got all the benefits. Avery waved him off.

James collected his books and left. He could feel Suzie staring at his back.

Lockers were two halls over. He stowed his books and headed for the parking lot.

Suzie was already there, leaning on his car. He turned in the doorway and went back in. *If I'm lucky, she didn't see me.*

The final bell rang, and the halls were suddenly filled with bodies and noise. Down the hall, he saw Slick talking to Drake.

Can't go that way. Friends could be more deadly than enemies sometimes. Letting on that he was hiding would be worse than confronting Suzie.

He turned towards the front offices. He could duck out that way. He toyed with the idea of faking another counseling session with Nurse Jameson, but dismissed it.

I need to just vanish until Suzie goes away.

James cocked his head to one side. *That's an idea.*

It was approaching four o'clock. Paris was seven time zones away. The girl might be home asleep at eleven PM, but if so, he could just transfer to the work shed at home and play with Grumpy for awhile.

Where do I want to be when I return? Outside the school, because they locked the doors as quickly as they could manage at the end of the day. Out of sight, of course.

There were a couple of pillars in the entrance. That would do.

55

Greg Archer entered the lobby of the Holiday Inn, and looked at the chart on the wall for the Lincoln conference room.

He entered. It looked very deserted.

I'm here at the right time. Is this the right Holiday Inn? The message left on his answering machine had been brief, and he could hardly understand the man with the distortion on the line.

"Gregory Archer?"

He looked around for the speaker, but there was no one there. He looked up at the public address speakers.

"Yes. My name is Archer."

"Have a seat." He did so. *That's the same voice, distortion and all.*

"I am in need of a sales representative who can travel extensively and deal with people of different nationalities."

"I can do that. What are you selling?" Archer decided to ignore the odd circumstances. Maybe it was a test.

"Unique high-tech services. We will get into that later. What I need to know first are your personal circumstances. Tell me about yourself."

Greg stifled the unease, and began to talk about himself. He was good at that. With no family left, he was free to spin a shiny, wholesome childhood in Ohio, and give good reasons why he didn't finish his degree at Purdue. The distorted employer wanted a salesman, so he concentrated on that part of his history. It wasn't as if he were a felon on the run, but he did have his share of failures, and he was used to carefully not-thinking about them. His successes were much more interesting, and he knew how to decribe them lovingly.

After a while, the voice asked him to take out his passport and thumb through the pages.

"What?"

"Humor me. Pretend there is a camera looking over your shoulder."

Archer glanced around, but could see nothing. *Do what the man said.*

He turned the pages. There were some good memories. It was amazing what images came back, just by looking at the round inked stamp of the Cayman Islands. He hadn't seen Connie in years, and where did he put his snorkel and flippers? But, most of the pages were still blank.

"You like the Caribbean?"

Archer jerked. It seemed like the voice was closer than the public address speakers. He looked around again, but there was nothing.

"Yes. I like it warm."

He put away his passport.

"Sir, could I ask what this is all about? This is the strangest interview I have ever seen."

"Can you agree to work for a non-US company?"

"I can work for anyone, I suppose." Doubts started nagging at him. "I can't do anything illegal."

"In international work, sometimes there are different laws in different areas. How do you define illegal?"

Uh oh. "Well, I suppose that some things are just crimes, no matter where you are. I wouldn't quibble about little stuff, but I couldn't work where people used guns. I'm a salesman. That's all I do."

"Good enough. What is your opinion of the Emperor?"

"The Emperor?" Suspicions started to crystallize. "Uh, you mean the one at the UN?"

"Exactly. He needs a salesman."

"The Emperor is a terrorist."

The voice laughed, and through the distortion, it sounded very strange indeed.

"Who has he terrorized? No one. However, the Emperor is sitting on technology that can completely revolutionize the world. He wants to sell unique services. The first year target is a billion dollars in sales. How does a ten percent commission sound?"

Greg Archer's mind skipped a track.

His voice rasped a little as he asked, "What are you selling?"

The Emperor listed a dozen different services.

"I will be working directly with you. Just like this—we won't be meeting face to face. I'll give you an assignment. You make the sale. I provide the services."

"And this isn't illegal?"

"There are hundreds of nations. Some will declare this commerce illegal, I suspect. It is new, different, and unsettling. You will always have the opportunity to turn down an assignment, if it exceeds your personal boundaries. I won't compel you to do anything."

Archer was already sold. He knew that the moment his vision of his bank balance began to blur.

"What do I do?"

56

James fell flat on the sidewalk. A man walked up and asked him something in high-speed French.

"Sorry," he muttered, and allowed the man to help him up.

"*Bonsoir.*" The man nodded and left.

I know that one. "*Bonsoir,*" he called back. *Good evening.*

He dusted off his jeans and looked down the darkened streets. *I don't see her anywhere. Did she lose her watch?*

There was a rumble beneath his feet. It wasn't until he spotted the Metro sign across the street that he put it all together. *She's on the subway. Dad's software strikes again.* He felt a shiver. If the teleportation sphere had materialized next to her, he would have slammed into the inside of a moving train car at high speed. *It could have killed me, and probably other people too.* The software had detected that, and moved him to the nearest clear, non-moving, location.

Thanks Dad.

Paris at night was cold. He was wearing his jacket, but it was easily ten degrees colder than Central Texas. He could see the Eiffel Tower in the distance, so to kill time and to keep moving, he headed in that direction.

There were a few places open, but most were closed.

He window shopped, attracted to a corner store that sold sexy clothes for women, like a Victoria's secret, but with all the fetish underwear out there on the city street for all to see. He checked to see if anyone was watching him and then went on.

If I'm so horny I get a kick out of that stuff, why am I running away from Suzie? He shook his head.

He turned a corner, as he realized the Eiffel Tower was not to his left. *This city is a maze.* It seemed that every building was exactly seven stories tall, and some of the streets were tiny. Hardly room for one car. Some he passed were parked up on the sidewalk.

He paused at a shop. There was a bank ATM machine in the wall, and inside looked like a tiny little bank. *A money exchange place.* There was a chart giving the exchange rates for several currencies. There were a lot of vacant lines on the chart.

They use euros now, and so do a lot of other countries. No need to exchange that money.

He felt in his pocket. Fifteen dollars, not enough to do much with, but it highlighted the fact that he didn't have the right money, even if there had been a store open at this time of night.

Just to drive the point home, the next corner had an open restaurant with a number of people eating and laughing. The railing went all the way to the edge of the street. He stepped off onto the pavement to go around, rather than walk through, among the tables.

I don't know the language. I wouldn't know what to say if anyone spoke.

Time to go home, I guess.

If I could face to the west and prepare myself, I'd bet I could avoid falling down.

But which way was west? The sky overhead was glowing with the reflected lights of the city, but there were no stars. It must be overcast.

He walked another block, and realized he was getting really close to the Eiffel Tower. It was a wide avenue and he could actually see more than just the storefronts.

He headed briskly towards the tower, and into a park.

The tower was imposing. He walked into the wide-open space beneath the legs. Closed ticket offices, he guessed.

Pilier Est. He looked over to the next of the four bases of the tower. *Pilier Sud.*

"Hmm." He walked over to the other side. *Pilier Nord.*

"Ah, ha!" He tried to pronounce "Pilier Ouest", but his tongue tangled in his mouth. *North, East, South, West. I hope they aren't just kidding.*

He trotted over into the trees, aligned himself *ouest* and pressed **ADJUST**.

Nothing happened. After a second's confusion, he pressed **LIGHT LIGHT LIGHT**. *There is a time out!* **ADJUST**.

It was like taking a missing step in the dark. He stumbled, but with a little dancing, managed to keep on his feet.

Home. He was in the deserted storage shed. The lights were off, but the sky was still light and he could see. He crept to the door. It was after sunset. *It's not midnight anymore.* The lights were on in the house, and he could see movement. His mother's car was in the driveway. *And my car is still at school.*

He pressed **ADJUST**. A little step and he was standing on gravel.

The place wasn't black. It was huge, a cave with a large hole in the ceiling with sunlight streaming in, and row upon row of computers.

Around the corner, he could hear someone walking.

In panic, he stabbed at his watch.

ADJUST. He fell clumsily against a brick wall. Was that Dad he had heard? He couldn't afford to take the risk.

He stood back up.

Back at school. Around the corner, he checked out the parking lot. His car sat alone.

I wonder how long she stayed?

Marketing

57

Greg Archer stumbled on his first step into Big Lake, Nevada. The Emperor had warned him. He stepped out of the shade of the Texaco station and glanced at his watch.

Leave it activated. He noted the time. Any time within the next thirty minutes and he could escape with one push of a button.

He paused in front of the storefront window. Hair was in place. Suit was straight. He hefted his briefcase and headed down the street.

It was a small town, and the city hall was smaller than the bait shop next to it.

Knock. Knock.

"Come on in."

The Mayor was relaxed at a small desk in the corner.

"Hello, there. Can I help you?"

Greg smiled. "Oh, perhaps. I was just admiring your town."

"We like it. Not much industry, though. Too dry to farm and too far from the interstate for a casino." The Mayor waved him to a chair.

Greg smoothly caught the name on a picture frame.

"Mayor Norris, I noticed that the bait shop seemed closed?"

"Oh not really. It's mine. If I hear a car drive up, I'll check it out. Do you want to some fishing gear? I have a good selection of Castaway's on sale."

Greg chuckled. "You don't expect I'd want to buy some bait?"

"Not unless you are headed towards Lake Mead."

"Where exactly is the 'big lake' in Big Lake?"

"That hill a few blocks over is the dam. But I'm afraid it is getting close to empty. Global warming or El Niño or something. It's been dropping for close to three years now. Come summer, unless something happens, the shallows'll get hot and the fish'll die."

Greg leaned forward in his chair. "Can't you get water from somewhere else?"

The Mayor shook his head and stuck his hands in his pants pockets. "I looked into it. Agricultural water is several hundred dollars per acre-foot. And that's only if you already have the canals in place.

"But with the Colorado River water crisis, there's no way we could get the state to help us. I'm worried about the wells. They're getting low too, and I'm not sure the city could afford to truck in water."

"Sounds like a tough place to be. What'll you do with no water?"

"Oh, I'll probably stay, but people are talking about closing down and moving."

Greg let the silence build.

"Well," he finally said, "there are other sources of water."

"What do you mean? Cloud seeding? We tried that."

"No."

"Well, what is it? I'm listening."

Greg picked up his briefcase. "Have you heard of the Emperor?"

He handed the Mayor a single sheet of paper.

"The Emperor can deliver water into the Big Lake reservoir at one dollar per acre-foot, or $10,000 per foot at your spillway, whichever you prefer. Payment due after delivery, one foot at a time. Dollars or imperials."

Greg closed the deal thirty minutes later. He had to guarantee it was legal, and was out on the dusty street quickly as he could manage.

Stepping back into his apartment a minute later, he was startled by his master's voice.

"How did it go?"

"Fine. Signed contract and everything. But boy he was needy! We could have charged ten times as much."

"I'm much more concerned with getting established. We're just getting our feet wet."

"He asked when do we start."

"I've already turned the water on. He should notice it soon enough."

Greg hesitated, then said, "You know, my commission will be a while showing up on this. I'll still need to pay my rent while we are getting established."

"Oh. How about a $20,000 advance? By the way your next assignment is on your kitchen table. I am re-programming your watch now."

"Fine," he whispered. He had been going to ask for a thousand.

58

The phone rang. Diana stepped into the kitchen and picked it up.

"Hello?"

"Hi, Beautiful."

"Bob! I'm so glad you called."

"I got your voicemail about the athletic banquet. Does James still want me to come home for that?"

"He is standing right beside me. Why don't you ask him yourself." She handed the phone to James.

"Hi, Dad. Can you come home for the athletic banquet?"

"Well, I don't know. Business is hectic right now, I don't know if I can make it."

On sudden impulse, James asked, "Then, can I come work for you?"

"Whoa, there. You're still in school. Besides the security here is pretty tight. I don't think it would be approved."

"I know a lot of stuff. You taught me to program. Or I could, you know, fetch stuff. I could be a go-fer."

"James. I know you are a good worker. If things were different, I'd love to have your help. It's just not practical right now."

James sighed. "I understand. Just keep me in mind. School will be out sooner than you think."

"Okay," he laughed. "I'll remember."

"Uh, Dad? Could you talk to Mom awhile? I think she gets lonely."

He handed the phone back, to his mother's bemused expression.

"Bob. I've missed you."

James headed towards his bedroom. He walked inside and faced east.

LIGHT LIGHT LIGHT
ADJUST

Being ready for it, he stepped into the french girl's bedroom without falling.

The light snapped on. She gasped.

She grabbed her blanket up to her neck.

James waved his hand, and immediately pressed his watch. He fell on his back as he returned to his father's work shed.

I wasn't ready for that. Was she naked? What time is it in Paris? What did she see?

No time.

He pressed the watch again, and feeling the curve of the earth in his step, speculated that he was farther north, but not too far west.

The base was lit this time, a bank of electric lights shone from near the computer consoles. He walked away from a rack of computers and surveyed the mass of gear in the stone gallery. There is no sound other than the whir of fans. He could hear his own footsteps, but if his father were still talking on the phone, then he was not here.

The Dwarves! Sitting in a row, looking very much dwindled and out of place among the imposing ranks of high powered computer racks, the old machines from the work shed were still powered up.

He logged in. The account was still active.

On a hunch he checked the cables, and located a single cable that has been sliced off, still dangling from an ethernet port.

This was the cable to home.

If I can only reconnect it!

He checked the software. As he expected, there was a transaction log. *It went dead on the eleventh or twelfth. I discovered it on the twelfth.*

And there it was, a log entry showing a sphere connection termination. There were details. *Great.*

He checked the sphere creation software. It was a little different than he remembered, but there was a place to enter the co-ordinates directly.

He typed fast. *Talk a long time Dad.*

Fine-tuning the tiny sphere's locations, he edged them both into the shadows behind the computers. He stuffed the cut cable back through to Texas and logged out.

ADJUST.

Diana Hill was still talking on the phone. James headed out to the work shed.

He located the crimp tool needed to put a connector back onto the cut cable.

Mom had been laughing.

As he worked, he thought, *It's been a long time since I've heard her laugh.*

59

ON SUSPECTE LA MAIN DE L'EMPEREUR DANS LA DÉLIVRANCE DE MINE AFRICAINE.

The tag line caught Oriel Meirieu's attention on a newsstand copy of Le Monde, as she headed for the Metro to work. She purchased a copy and read.

There had been a mine collapse in South Africa. Fifty miners had been trapped nearly a kilometer beneath the surface. After a day, with work crews struggling to reach them before their air ran out, an extraordinary event occurred.

The trapped miners walked out on their own.

According to their reports, a strange tunnel appeared glowing with sunshine. Hurriedly they had escaped, carrying their injured with them. Finding themselves in their own town, the mysterious tunnel vanished behind them.

Oriel nodded to herself. It sounded like the Emperor.

60

"Buzz! So it's you who called this meeting."

Buzz Chapman looked at Bill Gilbert and Earl Parker, two other vice-presidents for Western Petroleum.

"No, I thought one of you had called it."

The three executives looked at each other.

Parker shook his head. "Don't look at me. If my secretary tells me I have a meeting, I come."

"You don't suppose it's a computer glitch again?"

"I don't know."

There was a knock on the door.

A young man in an expensive suit entered. "I apologize for calling you here with no explanation. I know your time is valuable."

"Who are you?" asked Parker.

"I am a representative of the Emperor. I have come to make you a business proposition," said Archer.

Parker glanced at his watch. "I can listen for five minutes."

The salesman smiled. "More than enough I think. First a demonstration."

From his briefcase he took out two white plastic pipes, each an inch in diameter and two inches long, each capped on one end.

He tossed one over to Gilbert. "Would you hold that over the trash can? I'd hate to make a mess."

Puzzled, the executive did as he was told.

Archer took the other pipe and started pouring water into it from the pitcher sitting on the table.

The water ran out Gilbert's pipe and rattled into the trash can.

Chapman said, "Let me see that."

Archer took his over and handed the man the pipe and pitcher. The executive poured some water through, then set the pitcher down and poked his finger in the opening.

"Don't!"

Chapman jerked his finger out.

Archer chuckled, "I did the same thing when I first played with them. No damage to the finger," he held up his hand, "but I lost a couple of ounces of blood."

Parker growled, "What's the point of all this?"

"Simple. Cap off a large pipeline in say, Saudi Arabia. Cap off another in Houston. The Emperor will supply the magic, and you simply pump your Middle East oil directly to the Houston refinery. No oil tankers, with their attendant environmental dangers and costs."

"What diameter?" snapped Chapman.

Archer shrugged. "Up to six feet, I believe the Emperor said. Other arrangements could be made, I am sure."

"What does this cost us?"

"Twenty-five cents per barrel. Dollars or imperials."

The executives looked at each other. Gilbert mumbled, "A sixth the cost."

Parker asked, "What guarantees of performance does the Emperor supply?"

"None. In all honesty, the Emperor is above the law. Guarantees, contracts, court orders—they have no force over him.

"But he is interested in long term business arrangements. Try it out as a pilot program. You have nothing to lose. If it doesn't work, you haven't lost any oil."

Parker tapped his fingers on the table. "We would need an exclusive contract."

"Hmm. I'm not sure I am authorized to do that."

"No deal without an exclusive contract."

Archer spread his hands. "I will have to check with the Emperor on that."

An amplified, distorted voice came from somewhere near the ceiling. "One year."

Parker smiled. "Five years. We will need that long to sell our tankers."

"Three."

"Done."

61

"Jay, you got your FBI Emperor Task Force, and I'm still outside begging for crumbs."

"I'm sorry Rudy. I had the ear of Heisman, and he made good noises about you, but then we had a clamp-down."

"What happened?"

Jay was silent on the telephone. "Rudy, give me five minutes. I'll call you back. Let me see what I can do."

"Don't forget to remind them of the reams of data I have sent you."

"I won't."

Rudy waited. There was still quite a bit of information he was still digesting from Interpol's ICIS database. There had been reports of the Emperor making business deals in three countries so far, but the hotspot appeared to be in the USA.

I'd bet anything the Emperor is an American.

Ring.

"Rudy, here's the deal. Imperials started showing up in Seattle. Several different sources. The Bureau moved twenty agents into the area, but before we could turn up a lead, the sources dried up."

"You suspect a leak?"

"We don't know. But Heisman says I can send you a vetted summary of our meetings."

"Better than nothing. But I'm not giving up. I want a seat in your task force."

"Don't hold your breath. I can get you the summary in an hour, okay?"

Rudy poured over the carefully worded summary. Most names and places were excised.

One thing showed up immediately. Companies that had turned over the imperial bills to the police were now starting to claim them back. A market was developing for imperial script. E-bay was selling most of them. While they were selling at considerably less than parity with the dollar, the price was climbing.

The FBI had investigated some of the buyers. Some were collectors, or news media hungry to get their own copies to investigate.

But there were others. Some were secretive—there were more than a couple of buying agents working for clients who demanded anonymity.

One big buyer was the City of Los Angeles. When questioned, they reluctantly admitted that they had been contacted by a salesman who offered to reduce ozone levels on high smog days. He had offered a demonstration, and it had worked. They contracted for five more days, and imperials cost less than dollars, so they had gone out on E-bay to acquire them.

Rudy nodded. The Emperor was providing both supply and demand for his imperials.

The FBI had demanded to bug the drop and the city agreed.

He could see why the FBI wanted tighter security. There appeared to be several wonderful leads. Any cash or script that made it back to the Emperor was a fishing line they could use to reel him in. Any leak could spoil the whole deal.

62

"Yes, Coach."

"I've been meaning to talk with you about your grades. They were getting better. But now they seem to be sliding. I really want you on shot-put, this season, but if that French grade drops any lower, you'll be ineligible."

James nodded and made promises, but his heart wasn't really in it. Every day he checked the paper for articles about the Emperor.

What is the point of trying out for track? If Dad is the Emperor, or even just working for the Emperor, then the police will come for us any day now.

Still, his poorest subject was French, and he could do something about that.

When he got home, he went straight to the computer and activated the sphere program.

The software had changed again. There were more options than when he'd last used it. And those were more cryptic. This wasn't user-friendly software anymore. It had been streamlined and customized for a single user who had to do a lot of work in a short time on a tool he knew well.

But James knew the rough roadmap already, and the shortcuts were logical, once you figured them out.

I know one person in Paris. But she might not like it if I drop in on her again.

How about if I meet her in a safer place than in her bedroom?

He opened a monitoring window and switched to her location.

He was shocked when the image formed and zipped away. She had been riding the subway. *The Metro.*

Hmm. There had been an option....

He closed and restarted the monitor, only this time he clicked the TRKVEL option. *Track Velocity? I hope.*

This time her hand appeared in his monitor screen. The subway noise was still there, but he was tracking the velocity of her watch.

She'll see this. He moved quickly to the floor and under her seat. He contented himself with a nice view of her leg for the five minutes left of her ride.

There was a status window that gave co-ordinates and velocity. He watched it slow to a stop.

When his location started dancing around to the tune of her swinging arm, he disconnected from velocity tracking and shot up to street level and higher, where he could watch the people leaving the Metro station without being easily observed.

This is crazy. She's seen me before and she probably thinks I'm some kind of stalker. I shouldn't get anywhere near her.

She appeared on the stairs. Her coat was plain and dark, but her face—he recognized it in a flash.

It's just because she's the only person here I know.

She headed towards the river. James zipped ahead of her and found a spot where he could appear without being seen. Quickly he re-programmed his watch, adding the new location, and moved HOME into the second spot. He pressed **ADJUST**.

And fell on his rump.

Dusting himself off, he walked over to the cafe and sat down at a convenient table on the sidewalk and waited for her to walk up. *This is a stupid idea.*

He could see her from a block away.

She's beautiful. She was small, elfin. Suzie outmassed her a whole weight class, and Suzie wasn't fat.

His fingers fumbled towards his wristwatch. *This is crazy. I've gotta get out of here.*

Then she looked up. He waved.

She stopped in her tracks. Her face registered shock.

He smiled, waiting. What else could he do?

She glanced down the street, looking for anything suspicious. Hurriedly, she walked up to him and in French far too fast for him to follow, she asked him something.

104

"Whoa. I came here to learn French, but I don't know it yet."

She frowned intensely. "Quel est ... name?" She scanned his clothes. "American? Football?"

He nodded, and tapped his football jacket.

She pointed at him. "Vous êtes un ... spy ... pour l'empereur. Avec moi. Come."

He hesitated. She grabbed his hand and pulled him along. He found himself focusing on her touch, more than where she was dragging him. She was maybe a year or so older than he was, but he felt like he was being pulled along by a child.

A spy for the Emperor? Did he hear her correctly?

She could be taking him to the police. If so, he could just press his watch button and leave.

Dangerous. As soon as people know this isn't just an ordinary wristwatch, they'll be ready to shoot first.

He tugged back.

Where are we going? How do you say that in French?

"Où?"

She said "Soon."

Another block, and they entered a building. He noticed a man in an apron, and realized it was a restaurant.

The man greeted the girl and she led James to a table in the back.

She asked him something in more rapid-fire French, and he could only shake his head. She handed him a menu. He looked it over and realized he could understand some of the words. "*Poulet.*" He pointed to a chicken dish.

She ordered the meal and then asked him, "Pourquoi ... why ... were you in my bed?"

Bedroom. She means bedroom.

He struggled with his very limited French. And then gave up. "You are a beacon."

She shook her head.

"*Pourquoi êtes-vous à Paris?*"

"To learn French."

She was amused.

"*Mon nom est Oriel.*"

That one he knew. "*Mon nom est James.*"

"*Bonsoir James.*"

He grinned, and he knew he looked stupid.

"Why did you bring me here?" He waved at the restaurant.

Her smile dropped, and she looked at the door. "*C'est dangereux. La TV signale que l'empereur a été arrêté.*"

James couldn't follow. "Danger something ... what was the rest of that?"

"*L'Empereur* ... arrested."

"What?" He felt a spike in his chest. "I have to go."

She tried to keep him seated. He looked around the room at the other diners, paying him no attention.

"Oriel, thank you." He kissed her quick before he could change his mind, and then dropped down below the table and pressed **ADJUST**.

He rolled to his feet on the wooden floor of the work shed and headed into the house to check with CNN.

63

Rudy Ghest tapped Jay Russo's phone number with a smile on his face.

"Hello Jay. I've got a tape for you—if the FBI is still interested in cooperating with Interpol."

They called a meeting in a hurry.

Rudy stood up and addressed the Emperor Task Force.

"The President-for-Life of Eastern Chad presented this security tape to Interpol as a gesture of good will." There were some grumbles at that. President Nadjima was considered nothing more than a tribal thug.

"It has been obviously edited, but what is left is very interesting. Roll it."

A smiling salesman walked in escorted by a large black bodyguard who towered over him.

The President sat on a throne. "Who are you and why are you here?"

"I am the First Agent of Emperor of the Earth. I have been sent with an offer of service."

The scene shifted, a crude edit.

"This action will show to the world your great heart and give you an important advantage in world opinion over the rebels at your border.

"In return, the Emperor desires nothing more than Eastern Chad's recognition of the Emperor."

The President-for-Life listened carefully.

"What you say is interesting. However, it occurs to me that certain nations might be more grateful if I gave them an agent of this Emperor." He nodded to his bodyguard.

The salesman tried to run, but the bodyguard grabbed him up in a tight squeeze. They fell to the ground, and a second later, the two men went transparent and then vanished.

The President was screaming for his other bodyguards when the tape ended.

There was a agitation among the assembled agents.

Jay Russo asked, "Perry, how does this fit in with your theory that all the teleportation sightings were staged?"

64

Archer was sitting on the side of a bed, his coat off and looking beat.

"What happened then?" came a voice out of the air.

"I gave the whole spiel, right out of your playbook. The Emperor would move a mile-wide iceberg from the Antarctic into the desert near the refugee camps. Meltwater would solve the immediate drought problem and create an oasis there for agriculture that would persist for years. The President would hold a press conference taking credit for the humanitarian action and recognize Imperial rule.

"Right from the beginning, he didn't buy it. Maybe he doesn't understand the word 'humanitarian'. He sic'ed his bouncer on me and I was never so relieved when I was able to hit the switch on my watch. He had me in a bear hug and I was afraid I would pass out."

The voice said, "I'm sorry about that. I'm working on improvements to the system. How about a keyword you could shout that would trigger the abort as well?"

Archer checked the stiffness in his arm. "I'm not sure I'm up for this kind of pitch. I'm a salesman, not a politician."

"It's what you signed on for. It's not just your commission check this time. I've already got your Grand Cayman portal set up."

Archer grinned, "You know how to dangle a carrot."

Then he frowned, "What happened to the other guy?"

"Don't worry about him. He passed out in the gas chamber just as fast as you did. He's my problem."

Archer nodded. "It's just ... this is the first time it's turned nasty."

"And I'm sorry I put you in danger. And I'm sorry I need you to go to plan B."

"So soon? I'm a mess."

"We need to move fast. CNN has the story. There's even a nice video clip of you."

"Oh, my." Archer felt a sinking feeling. He had been working at a furious pace for the past two weeks, making a couple of deals a day. It had almost started to feel like a real, but high-stress, job.

But now, people knew his face and would be hunting for him. And not to get his autograph either.

He was getting used to the Emperor's voice. Either that or the distortion had been turned down. "Yes, the world now has a face to put on the Imperium. If you had doubts before, now's the time to get rid of them. If I'm the Emperor of Earth, then you are a protected diplomat. If I'm just a crazy man with a gadget, you are just a crook's henchman."

65

Ngarta Habre, bodyguard for President Nadjima, woke on the beach, aching and hungry. It was hot and very humid. He stripped to the waist and wandered along the shoreline, looking for any sign of another human being.

There were palm trees, with coconuts. And surely there were fish in the sea, but without fresh water he would die.

When he turned back and started checking in the other direction, he quickly discovered a small creek, wide enough to step across, but containing cool fresh water.

Shortly on the tail of that discovery, above the high-tide mark, he found a couple of yellow packages, stamped with the UN globe symbol and 'World Food Organization'. He tore it open. Biscuits. He ate the entire first package, and felt energy returning.

Food, water, shade. He would live, but how long would he be trapped here?

66

James watched the CNN coverage, wondering, with the rest of the world, who was the man who vanished before the security cameras.

It's not Dad. He'd never been so relieved to find that Oriel had been wrong when she said that the Emperor had been arrested.

But for the first time, people could see the vanishing act. News commentators were confidently using the word 'teleportation' in their reports. One reporter said 'beamed away', but that had stopped over an hour ago.

Star Trek had given the idea to the world, but there weren't any sparkles. Now news commentators were talking to physicists and science fiction writers about what it all meant.

James put a bag of popcorn in the microwave and sat down to watch the news for as long as he could.

One of the writers being interviewed gave a list of novels that talked about the societal implications of teleportation. And James wrote down the names.

What did it mean to the world that teleportation existed?

What does it mean to me? The world doesn't have it yet, just the Emperor and me.

He glanced at the clock and realized it was midnight. That would make it 7 AM in Paris.

I could go back and have breakfast with her. If she still wanted to talk to him. He'd vanished when they were at dinner. He hoped she'd been able to pay for it.

If he wanted to talk to her, then he should at least be able to pay for her breakfast. He checked his cash box. But they didn't use dollars over there. It was euros.

How could he get some euros?

There had been that money exchange place.

He started the sphere program and after a few minutes, he located a different money exchange shop.

He re-programmed his watch and went to Paris. The shop had just opened and the man behind the counter spoke English. He traded his small stash of dollars for euros. They were interesting, different colors and sizes.

He moved out of sight and pressed **ADJUST**.

"Oriel." He appeared behind her.

"Eek!" She jumped and turned to face him. *"Un moment s'il vous plaît."* She wrapped her arms about herself and dashed into another room.

James realized she didn't think she was dressed properly, but it'd been okay by him. She wasn't by any means naked. *Is this one of the 'societal changes' of teleportation? Will everyone have to be fully dressed all the time?*

She opened the door, in a dark dress.

"Bonjour James."

He nodded. *"Bonjour Oriel. Vous aimez aller déjeuner. J'ai des euros."* He had practiced how to invite her to breakfast, but he wasn't at all sure of the accent.

"Oui. Merci." At least she understood.

She led the way to a sidewalk cafe and James discovered French pastries. He loved the strawberry ones. He supplied the cash, but counting change he left to her.

Oriel was stern, *"N'héritez pas mon appartement comme cela. J'ai été embarrassé."*

The translation was beyond him, but he got the meaning. Don't drop in on her like that again.

I guess I won't mention the time I saw her in the shower.

He tried to phrase a response, then threw up his hands.

"Only in an emergency, I promise. Otherwise I will knock."

He smiled. Her forehead wrinkled most charmingly as she struggled with the English.

"Ok. Une urgence."

She was eager to know anything about the Emperor. She knew from the stories on the news that he was interested in the needy. The government had called on the populace to report anything strange, but indignantly, she said she saw nothing bad in the Emperor.

"Pourquoi devez-vous apprendre le français? N'y a-t-il pas des agents français de l'empereur?"

"Talk slower, please." He didn't want to give the wrong impression. "No English agents. No French agents. No Russian agents. Not yet.

"L'Empereur desire des agents français, but he has to be cautious." He knew he mangled it.

But she nodded. He could tell she wanted badly to believe that the Emperor knew how important the French were.

He remembered something Coach Barlow said. He tried to rephrase it in his own words.

"L'Empereur is the emperor of all de monde. He knows the French have been important players on the international stage for centuries, and he is looking for honest people who can be des agents français."

She put her hand on his arm and with an earnest gazes she said, *"Je ferai n'importe quoi aider l'empereur."*

He didn't need to translate it. The meaning came through instantly. She would do anything to help the Emperor.

67

Clang! Clang! Clang!

The sound of a great bell echoed over the refugee camp on the border of Eastern Chad and the Sudan.

A voice, amplified but recognizable to all echoed over the makeshift shelters.

"This is General Ahmat of the Democratic Rebellion against the demon Nadjima. The Democratic Rebellion has negotiated with the Emperor of the Earth to provide water for the suffering people of Eastern Chad. The Emperor desires that no one should be hurt and prayerfully begs all to stay away from the new mountain until noon."

Acyl Terap was at the south edge of the camp. As the echoes of the voice died away, he noticed a wavering in the air, and a cool breeze. Over the dunes, a haze a mile wide and hundreds of feet tall appeared. He started to turn and run, but the breeze compelled him. It tasted wet.

That wasn't a sandstorm. He moved closer.

A white mountain appeared. It appeared to grow out of the mist.

No. The mist is going away.

The air echoed with sharp cracks, like rifle shots. Foot by foot, the mist receded, revealing the mountain, unlike anything he had seen.

Other refugees were shouting behind him, coming his way.

I have to get there first. That was the rule of the refugee camp. When the foreigners brought food and water, only the quick ones ate.

He ran, just ahead of the crowd. With each step, the mountain appeared more strange and more fearful.

There was another *crack*, and a cliff broke free and shattered to the ground.

Acyl was hit by a rock. It was blue, and it burned to the touch. He picked it up. Wetness trickled over his hand. He licked.

"Water! It is water!"

The growing crowd took up the chant, and rushed to gather the pieces.

A sharp crack sounded, and another large chunk fractured from the cliffside. Shards and frigid air blasted them. Shrieks and cries of pain were heard among the mist, but no one stopped gathering the precious cargo.

68

James sat with the rest of the football team, chatting about school. The Volunteer Fire Hall was filled to capacity. All the players of all the teams, plus their families were there for the Athletic Banquet. But the athletes had their own tables up front. Some of the cheerleaders sat beside their boyfriends.

James noticed Suzie trying to catch his eye, but he avoided eye contact. There were others here at the table with much more claim on her and he honestly didn't care to get on her roller coaster again.

I could have invited Oriel, but wouldn't that have been a disaster? Even if she had been just from another school, putting the local girls in the shade would make him a lot of enemies.

Coach Barlow had caught him in class rattling off correct French responses and questioned him about his much-improved accent.

"J'avais pratiqué dans les laboratoires de langue." He had said, but he wasn't sure she believed him.

He had eaten out five times with Oriel now. Even his sleep schedule was getting messed up, as he took an early evening nap and then woke up at midnight to have breakfast with her at a little place on Rue Malar, just a few blocks from the River Seine.

He knew a lot about her now. She worked at La Samaritaine, a huge department store overlooking the Seine, saving up for college tuition at EPITA, some kind of computer school.

With Oriel on his mind, the events of the Athletic Banquet were not as important as he had thought they would be. His season had been cut short, and he had no delusions about his statistics or placing in the Central Texas regional standings.

It was just a time to listen to his buddies and wonder what would happen to all of them in the near future. In the wrong hands, or even in too many right hands, teleportation would destroy the culture. He'd picked up one of those novels in the library, one where people kept their women and treasures constantly hidden behind mazes so that teleporters couldn't get in to rape and loot. But not even that solution made sense with the spheres. *I could steal anything in the world, as long as I had a vague idea of where to look.*

The steak dinner came to a halt and the coaches began giving out awards. He was called to the stage, as part of the team. Individually, the coaches bragged on them. Coach Avery claimed great things for him in his senior year. At one time, he would even have believed it.

Dad! There was his father, sitting with his mother. He had his airline suitcase and one of the cooks was bringing him a plate. James waved, and his father waved back.

After the ceremony, he rushed back to join his family.

"I didn't know if I were going to make it or not," he said between bites. "I just finished a really huge project and I needed to refresh my energy anyway, so I took a last minute flight. I'll have to go back tomorrow, but it's worth it to see you up there."

"You took a taxi here, and you need a ride home," James supplied, relieving his father of having to make up a story. "Can I drive you?" His parents exchanged a look and he said "Yes."

There were other people who were pleased to see Bob, and it took another thirty minutes before they were ready to leave.

"How are your projects going?" James asked, once they were in the car.

"Oh pretty well. I can't tell you much. Security, you know."

"I thought so. It's good to have you home. I've got so much to tell you."

"Oh?"

"Yes." James tried to make school sound interesting. It was hard.

"We were going to listen to the French President's speech at the UN, but saw the Emperor's announcement instead. That was a blast. You never saw so many politicians running around looking confused at one time.

"Dad, what do you think about the Emperor? Is he a crook?"

His father looked out the window for a moment.

"The way the world works, if he succeeds—if he avoids being caught or killed, then he is indeed Emperor of the Earth and everything he's doing is legal.

"But if he's captured, then he is just a crook.

"All the royal houses in the world came into being by force of arms. A man with the will to rule and the skill to survive became legal when the others gave up and acknowledged his claim. If the nations of the earth can't stop the Emperor, then he is who he claims to be. It's just a battle of will."

James nodded, then added, "I've met a girl."

"Anyone I know?"

"No. I just met her this week. She's a big fan of the Emperor. Apparently there are quite a number of people who see him as the defender of the weak. She's said that when the Emperor is in need of a French-speaking agent, she wants to join up."

His father chuckled. "That would be pretty dangerous."

"Why?"

"Because I don't think the Emperor will survive. After all, he is just one man against the whole world."

"But he has teleportation! And isn't there more than just one man? What about that man in Eastern Chad?"

His father nodded. "Yes, he probably has an agent or two working for him. But still, even with all the automation in the world, he can't be everywhere. A hundred unskilled minds can probably beat one man with a million computers. At the least, the Emperor has to sleep sometime."

James frowned. "Then why would he do it? The Emperor could have kept a low profile for years, for a whole lifetime maybe, and still be rolling in wealth. Why did he announce himself to the world? 'Hey look at me! I'm King of the Hill! I dare you to knock me off.'"

"He must have had a reason. A reason worth his life."

James nodded. *He's trying to protect us. If we don't know anything, then we aren't accomplices.*

Too late.

Other questions bubbled up in James. "I've been wondering. The son of the king is a prince, but what about an emperor. What do they call his son? An emplet?"

Bob shook his head and chuckled. "I'm not really sure. It all varies by which nations have the Emperor. I think it's still a prince, or maybe a crown prince. We'll have to ask the Emperor when he is acknowledged."

69

"Are you from the Dean's office?" asked Professor Keith Rutherman. He put down his wrench and climbed out from behind the metal supporting structure.

Archer smiled, "No. I represent someone who would like to invest in your research, Dr. Rutherman."

"Oh?" He looked closer at the man in the suit. "Do I know you?"

"Perhaps. Have you heard of the Emperor?"

Light dawned on the physicist's face.

"What does he want with me?"

"Personally, I don't know. My science classes left off at pulleys and inclined planes. However, the Emperor would like to fund your research. He suggests a five year contract at a funding rate initially double what you have now."

Rutherman sat down. "Does the Emperor even know what I am working on?"

Archer pulled a notepad from his pocket. "You are working on 'plasma confinement using Bellerman space'."

"How does he know that? I haven't published yet."

"The Emperor, in my experience, knows everything. Perhaps he has read your working notes. He can, you know."

Rutherman looked pale. "Teleportation. Yes, I had heard that, but I didn't believe it. Is he an alien?"

"From outer space? No. I talk to him all the time. He's human."

Rutherman's mind raced over the offer. Funding was drying up, especially for untried, off the beaten path, confinement techniques.

"What would the Emperor want in exchange?"

Archer flipped in his notepad. "The Emperor wishes you to concentrate on increasing the plasma temperature and density, with the goal of fusion energy production."

Rutherman nodded. That was what he was trying for already.

Archer continued, "It would be understood that all working notes are open to the Emperor's eyes. And that all papers for publication be submitted to the Emperor for permission."

The physicist sagged. "I was afraid of that. I don't think that I can agree to a restriction on publication."

Archer nodded, still reading. "The Emperor believes, from his own sources, that if the paper you are currently writing is submitted to peer review, that it will be forwarded by the DOE to the NSA and that you will be prohibited from publishing it. The government may provide you with additional funding, but that's not certain.

"If you continue with your current line of research, the Emperor is confident that full publication will be impossible. He offers you the only alternative to working under Defense Department supervision and control."

Dr. Rutherman nodded. "I have a friend who had that happen. I didn't realize I was close to the line."

"There are decided military ramifications to your research. The Emperor is more interested in cheap energy for the masses than a way to power warships. He wants to help, but unless you limit your paper, you will quickly lose control of your working environment."

Archer put down his notebook. "If I can put in a personal note, he's a good employer."

"Okay." Rutherman sighed. "Where do I sign?"

Archer reached into his pocket. "You don't need to sign anything. Just cash this check. It's your first quarter's budget."

70

Rudy sat quietly through the FBI taskforce meeting. He avoided asking too many questions. Agent Heisman could exclude him in an instant, so he hesitated to make waves.

The three payoffs they'd bugged had produced nothing. The money, the imperials, and the hidden radiotracers had just vanished without a trace. One of them had been a high-powered beacon like those used by crashed aircraft. The signal could be picked up by satellite from anywhere on the earth. None of them produced anything.

The bills had all their serial numbers recorded and all banks were notified. Nothing yet.

One of the officers joked about dusting the money with anthrax, but it was tagged as a bad idea all around.

Reports of missing items were dwindling, whether from reduced activity or from the desire to hang onto the imperial script. The FBI had gained a reputation for confiscating the payment.

Russo said, "We should just pay face value for them. Announce it to the world."

Heisman shook his head. "We don't have the budget for that, and orders from the top are to do nothing to give the Emperor any appearance of legitimacy."

Rudy made his contribution.

"The new oasis in Eastern Chad is getting a lot of attention. Military forces are collecting on both sides of the border. Estimates are that the ice will take years to completely go away. Sand dunes are already burying some of the ice and experts predict that it will provide a reservoir that could last for decades.

"A lot of people are watching this carefully. There is growing interest in doing business with the Emperor."

He clicked the slide projector. It showed a newspaper.

"The New York Times has started a special section in the classified ads. The section title is simply 'For the Emperor' and it is getting quite popular. It's like letters to Santa Claus. Anyone who wants the Emperor to do something for them can buy a simple ad and include it here.

"There isn't any evidence the Emperor actually reads these, but I would like to draw your attention to the circled ad.

"The phone number is international. Algeria. Interpol has determined that the Algerian government is attempting to strike a deal with the Emperor to create iceberg oases for them. Such a deal would presumably include recognition of the Emperor's claim to power."

There was a mutter of dismay around the table.

"They can't do that."

Rudy glanced at the distinguished looking older man who had spoken. He had no name badge. *Who are you to say what another nation can do?* But he kept his mouth shut.

Rudy continued, "While this is interesting, I suggest that we could turn this communication channel to our advantage."

Politics

71

Archer walked into the offices of the Washington Post. He asked for a meeting with Georgia Urman. He was almost turned away before someone recognized who he was.

The famous reporter slowed from her run as she hurried into the conference room. A photographer was on her heels.

"Hello, my name is Gregory Archer, First Agent of the Emperor. I was wondering if you would care to interview me?"

Georgia Urman introduced herself "Yes, certainly. Have a seat. May we take a couple of photographs first?"

Archer smiled. "Yes, that would be prudent, wouldn't it."

The photographer quickly knelt, putting the camera even with his face. His camera clicked away several times a second. Urman waved him off.

She had her recorder running.

"Mr. Archer. Why have you come to talk to us?"

"It was the Emperor's idea. My face has already become public and there's no sense in trying to hide my identity any more. You were chosen because of your reputation. If the Emperor is satisfied with the final copy, then perhaps there will be more chats."

The interview was off and running.

Archer related his hiring, and the interesting facts of his work.

"I've never seen the Emperor, but we've had many conversations. I personally have no doubt he's an American, very intelligent, and honestly committed to establishing his legitimate claim to his title."

All of his commissions for the Emperor had been relatively simple contracts for goods or services. He made the sale, and the Emperor handled the delivery and pickups.

"For example, the City of Los Angeles has contracted to relieve serious smog build-up over the city."

"How could he do that?"

"It's a simple matter of opening a teleportation gateway from one part of the world to another. He could open a gate thousands of feet in diameter and let a high-pressure weather center over Nebraska, or the Pacific, or Timbuktu for that matter blow the contaminated air out over the ocean."

The reporter nodded, "I understand. And how about the payment?"

Archer chuckled. "That is interesting. The Emperor tells the customer where to leave the payment, in dollars or imperials, and he picks it up at his leisure.

"It only gets interesting when the FBI gets involved, like they did in LA."

"What did the FBI do?"

"They included a radio tracer with the payment. Always trying, those FBI guys. But the Emperor has procedures that protect him from that sort of thing."

"How did the Emperor contact you in the first place?"

"I read an employment ad in the paper."

"Was it the New York Times?"

"No, why?"

She told him of the 'For the Emperor' column and asked if the Emperor read them.

"I don't know for sure, but the Emperor seems to know everything. I half expect that I am personally under constant surveillance."

She scribbled away.

"Doesn't the lack of privacy bother you?"

"Maybe at the very first. But you know, the world is changing.

"Privacy and private property are illusions in the day of teleportation. I've learned to live with it, and I believe that the man in control, my Emperor, is an honest man."

The phone rang. It was answered by the photographer and handed to Urman.

She looked at Archer. "It seems that police are approaching the building."

He nodded and vanished.

72

Harris Barr yelled, "Get the satellite phone set up!"

He sweated as he dug his camera bag out from under the collapsed masonry. When the earthquake hit, he had dashed for safety outside, but'd forgotten to bring his camera.

There it was. He jerked it free and headed outside.

Ken had the headphones on and unfolded the dish.

Harris began sweeping the scene with his camera, talking all the while into the microphone.

"This is Harris Barr, CNN in Erzincan Turkey, reporting on a devastating earthquake. I estimate it at over seven on the Richter scale. In this part of town, as you can see, nearly every building has collapsed. People everywhere are rushing to check for survivors."

It was a long afternoon. They wandered through the streets, keeping the world updated while the locals did what they had done throughout history, dig in the rubble for their loved ones.

"As we reported last time, the sun is going down, and with it, the hopes for finding survivors. There is no power for lights, and without light, the search cannot continue.

"What!"

The reporter stuttered on camera, as a brilliant flash lit the sky.

"What was that? Pardon me, but a huge light has just swept across the sky, like..."

He went silent as the sky lit up, and stayed lit.

He frantically got the camera aimed high.

"This is Harris Barr, and something amazing has happened here in Erzincan Turkey. The moon has grown enormous, lighting the landscape."

He faltered for words. It was the moon, obviously the moon, with craters and everything, but it covered half the sky. It was bright enough that he raised his hand to shelter his eyes.

A shout echoed through the city, and searchers returned to their task of pulling the living from the rubble.

73

Ngarta Habre was bored with his life on the island. Every day, UN food packets arrived from an invisible hole in the sky, but he tired of the monotonous food and began fishing with a sharpened stick.

He stared at his feet, resting in the cooling waters of the creek.

Today, I will follow the water.

He put on his shoes, and cut a walking stick.

The island wasn't large, and it was the weakling brother to the tropical paradise he had seen so often on TV. The palm trees only grew in the one bay where he had awakened. The other side of the island was mostly shallow pools, flooded regularly by the tides. If it weren't for the creek and the food drops, no large animal could survive here.

The creek wound through thick cane breaks, and sometimes he had to break through them by brute force. His knife was no machete.

Every step turned the clear water to mud. There was something wrong with this creek. He'd sensed it before, but he couldn't make sense of what he saw.

Until he broke through the last of the cane.

In the center of the island, the rock he had seen vaguely in the distance was no normal volcanic outcropping.

It was a huge, perfectly round ball of granite, a hundred feet high, sunk a third of its height into the mud.

From the very top of this impossible ball, clear cold water trickled down its side, and splashed as a wide shower to the ground.

Ah. This is no ordinary creek. This Emperor has made it.

He circled the ball at a distance.

On the other side, near the top, there was a pit in the perfect ball. Large enough for a man, it looked perfectly round—as perfect as the ball itself. High and unreachable, there was a word painted on the stone in yellow.

EXIT

74

James munched a croissant. "I told him about you."

Her eyes brightened, "You didn't! What did you say?"

James had realized the language practice was a success a couple of days before, when he found that he was no longer translating. Sometimes Oriel spoke English, and sometimes French, as did he. They were always explaining new words, but they were no longer struggling. They just talked.

"Only that I knew a girl, who spoke French, and who was interested in being an agent for the Emperor."

"What did he say?"

"Not much. He has to be very cautious in letting people into his service. Don't expect things to happen fast. But don't worry, I'll keep reminding him."

She pouted and then brightened. "Many times a man will say things to impress a girl, and one has to be cautious. But then, I remind myself of what I have seen with my own eyes."

James felt the faintest twinge of guilt. He was exaggerating, but in his heart, he knew his father was the Emperor.

"Sometimes, a man has to be careful too, when a girl looks at him just so. He may promise more than he can deliver. A man will do much to see that hero reflected in her eyes."

She blinked, and looked away.

"Did you see what he did in Turkey? He brought the Moon to Earth."

James laughed. He had seen the CNN reports, and had gone immediately to the computer to scan the logs. He was getting adept at that.

"Hardly that. The Emperor collected the light from close to the moon and brought that close to Turkey. They needed light, and that was the only way."

She nodded. Maybe she even understood. "Why the moon? Why not bring sunlight?"

James shook his head. "It wouldn't have worked." He picked up the salt and pepper shakers. "The sunlight was coming this way," he illustrated with his hands. "Turkey was already on the night side. Teleportation can collapse distance, but it can't change the angles. Letting sunshine through would just cast a searchlight up into the sky. They needed light on the ground. He had to get light coming in the right direction—the reflected light from the moon."

She frowned as she worked it out. "I think I understand. I didn't know that—about the angles."

"Oh yes, every time I step into Paris, I have to be careful stepping over the seven time zones worth of distance or I will fall flat on my face. It took practice to learn that trick."

75

Archer complained. "This isn't working out like I had hoped."

The Emperor's voice asked, "The fame?"

"Notoriety is closer to the fact. My new house is nice, and I love the scuba, but I am always just on the edge of discovery. Grand Cayman is too modern and connected. Everyone has seen my face by now on television. I'll never be able to walk the street or meet the neighbors."

"There are other places to live. Places where people don't watch TV."

"Places without indoor plumbing, you mean?"

"That, and places where people don't care about international politics. I'm sure with a little research you can come up with something."

"What do you do?"

"Other than never let my face be seen, or my voice be heard without distortion? Other than living like a hermit and experiencing life through a computer screen?"

"Yes," Archer laughed, "other than that."

"I'm still working on it. Getting some stable nation to recognize me legally would do a great deal."

"Yeah. It's a bummer about the terrorist thing."

"Right." Even through the distortion, Archer could hear the Emperor's anger. Being listed as an international terrorist might do that to you.

"What are you going to do about it?"

"I have plans in motion. I told the UN at the beginning. I would be good to my friends. Now they are going to have to be shown what I do to my enemies."

"The USA?"

"Yes."

Archer was disturbed.

"I'm an American, you know."

"So am I, but don't tell anyone. Oh yes, you already did." The Emperor chuckled. "Don't worry. I'm not a terrorist. They made a political move against me. I'll make a political move back."

76

"Lady Emilia Burton."

Emilia dropped the plate she was drying. It shattered on the floor.

The voice from nowhere continued. "My apologies for startling you."

Her hands shook, but she quickly dried them and calmed herself.

"Not at all. I wasn't really expecting you to contact me."

The voice shifted slightly in pitch and distortion. "Are you still looking for a job as an executive assistant? Your credentials look admirable."

She sat down on a kitchen stool. "Yes. Although to be honest, I chose the Emperor's column in the Times because I knew a lot of people would be reading it."

"Would you still consider working for me?"

"Oh yes."

"You do know that the United States has placed me on a list of terrorists in order to discourage people from doing business with me. Britain has reciprocal agreements with the US on these matters."

"What would I be expected to do?"

"For the next few months at a minimum, you would read the 'Letters to the Emperor' published in the Times and other London papers. Using your best judgment, print out a summary of the most interesting and deserving—a daily top five. You would put this report in your desk drawer and I would retrieve it.

"I can pay a flat rate, or a commission on business proposals that come from items you locate."

"Is that what you want? Business contacts."

"Partly. There is a class of services only I can provide. Whether business, or charity, or magic tricks for a child's birthday party—unless you can find them, I can never be of service.

"Business provides the money which will pay you, but I have many goals."

77

The Secret Service jumped into action, the instant the large white package with a red ribbon around it appeared in the Oval Office. The President had taken a step toward the package, but was instantly snapped up by his bodyguards and rushed to the elevator.

He was deep in the secure room below in seconds, while bomb experts were being rushed to the site.

The letter attached to the package was carefully removed and checked for chemical or biological contamination.

The bomb squad's level of stress went up a notch when a Geiger counter reported radiation. The package was scanned carefully by the most sophisticated detectors before being gently hoisted on a platform and carried out to a bomb disposal truck and then to a nearby military base.

The President was shown a video scan of the letter, still in its quarantine. He was soaking up the content, when a phone call from the Washington Post came in.

"We have received a message from the Emperor, reporting that a package was delivered today to the President of the United States, containing the following message:

"'Those who create false terrorist warnings for their own political ends must have only themselves to blame for their fears. Attached are three items of deactivated ordinance. The most powerful nations on the earth may use their power only at Imperial discretion.'

"We at the Post would like confirmation of these events and we would like to know what the three items of ordinance were."

78

"You may not feed this information back to Interpol until there is a presidential release."

Rudy nodded, "I understand. That's been a part of Interpol since the beginning. Unless we earn your trust, you won't tell us anything."

He listened carefully to the report. The full details were to be kept strictly limited. The news media reports already had the broad outline, but the ordinance details were sensitive.

Agent Heisman gave the details himself.

"The first, and most dramatic item, was the trigger from a hydrogen bomb."

There were whistles and grunts of amazement from the agents.

"This had been a small plutonium device, a bomb in its own right, which when exploded would have set off the hydrogen bomb riding in the warhead of a Pershing missile. Serial numbers confirm that the Emperor had removed this trigger from a submarine still at sea.

"It had been deactivated in two forms. One, the chemical explosive shell that would have driven the plutonium to criticality had its igniters removed. The second was more significant—the plutonium itself had been riddled with holes like a swiss cheese. Enough plutonium had been removed so that it would never have gone critical.

"This last was not detectable except by x-ray or ultrasonics. It is possible that there are other nuclear weapons in the field that have been rendered inoperable. Every one of them will have to be inspected.

"The second item was a mortar shell. Serial numbers confirm it had vanished from stores in a NATO warehouse in Germany. Externally, it looked perfect. However, a careful disassembly showed that the propellant charge had been contaminated with mineral oil. A test firing of a dummy shell with that propellant failed to ignite. The shell had been converted undetectably into a dud.

"The third was an anticlimax. A single 7.62-mm rifle shell was also contaminated in the same way as the mortar shell. It was also a dud.

"The demonstration by the Emperor appears to be that the whole range of our weapons systems can be deactivated at will, and in a fashion that is undetectable by our current procedures. It is important that these details be kept closely guarded lest our opponents believe that it has already been done and that we are defenseless."

One of the FBI men asked, "Why did the Emperor give the message to the press? It seems to be a reaction to the terrorist listing. But now, everyone knows he set a bomb on the President's desk. That confirms he is a terrorist."

Rudy said, "Maybe. It's a message that he *can* be a terrorist, and a very effective one, the moment he chooses. But it is also a message to those in the know that he can trump whatever we can do against him. The terrorist listing was a public attack on the Emperor's image. But as I read the news accounts, the general public does not feel threatened. Only people like us, with the full knowledge of the facts, are having the shakes.

"Day by day, there are more reports of the Emperor doing this or that rescue, or bringing water to the desert or bringing that unseasonable rain over Montana's forest fire.

"The people love him. They don't understand the threat he is."

The man with no badge grumbled, "We really only have two courses open to us. Change people's perception of him—play up the terrorist aspects of the Emperor, or find him and shut him down."

79

Knock. Knock.

James looked up from his homework. *That's the front door. Strangers.*

The driveway was at the south end of the house and everyone they knew came to the back door as a matter of course.

He looked at the clock. *Mom isn't due for another fifteen minutes.*

He closed the book and walked to the door.

Two men in suits were standing there.

"Good evening." They displayed FBI badges. "I am Agent Lambert and this is Agent Rickey. We would like to speak to Robert Hill."

Don't think.

"He's not in town right now. What do you want with him?"

"We just want to ask him some questions. Is your mother at home?"

James glanced at his watch. He had to fight the impulse to hide it from their sight. *It's just a normal watch.*

"She should be here in ten or fifteen minutes."

"We will wait then."

James looked them over again. "I can't let you in. There's the porch swing or you can wait in your car." He closed the door.

When he saw them through the window heading back toward their car, he made a dash to his room.

His fingers were jittery as he opened a new monitor sphere and attached it to the wristwatch of one of the agents. He closed the monitor down immediately—he couldn't risk it being noticed.

Then he located the 'Bail' program and set it on a timer.

In one hour, it would sever the connection and wipe the evidence of the sphere program.

Voices came from the living room.

She's early!

His mother had invited them in. Panic in his mind, he turned off the computer's monitor and sat paralyzed in his chair.

They're going to get me. They know it's Dad. How can I alert him?

"James!" His mother called him.

He picked up his school notebook and pen and forced himself to calm down. *Walk slow.*

The agents were seated on the couch, and his mother was trying to talk them into having a coke or coffee.

"James, when was the last time you talked to your father?" she asked.

"After the banquet, that night. You had already taken him to the airport when I went off to the track meet the next morning."

The agent asked, "What did you talk about?"

"Stuff. School. What I was going to do next year in football. Politics—you know, the Emperor stuff."

Both agents reacted slightly to that.

"What brought up that subject?"

"Oh, I did." He explained about the French class video.

"What did your father say?"

"Oh, not much. He expected the guy to get caught. A manpower thing."

There were many more questions. They seemed ready to stay all evening.

"Mrs. Hill, where do you think your husband is, and what is this project he is working on?"

Her hands were jittery, and she had a handkerchief knotted up between her fingers. "You asked me that before. I don't know anything more that I've already told you!"

She rubbed her head. "I've had a long day at work, and I can't think straight anymore. I think you should leave."

Agent Lambert nodded. "I understand. We would like you to come into town tomorrow morning where we can finish this up."

Diana was about to complain, when he handed her a card.

"This is the address. Please be there at 9 AM. There is a parking lot to the side of the building."

She stared at the card. "Okay. Fine. Just go now."

By the time they were gone, his mother was crying and James felt very trapped.

80

He desperately wanted to rush to the computer and open an audio tap to the FBI's wristwatch, but his mother needed comfort. Taking just a second to deactivate the timer on the 'Bail' self-destruct, he came back to the kitchen and re-heated the supper she had brought home. He talked with her through the meal.

All the worries she had put aside about her husband were now out open and raw. James tried to keep cool.

"The FBI are just fishing. Dad is the most honest man I know. Whatever they're looking for—it just has to be a mistake."

When she finally went to bed, he opened the connection to Agent Lambert. The man was still working, in some office. James made the spy portal as tiny as he could and snooped around the office. Shortly, Lambert finished work on his report and closed down his laptop. James ached to know what it said, but he didn't know how to find out.

When the lights went out, James made sure that the Lambert's watch tracker was working, but he kept a second open portal in the office, trying to read whatever materials were left open on the desk, in spite of the low light. He dared not shine his own light through the portal. They might have spy cameras of their own in the office.

One thing caught his attention. Scribbled on a notepad were the words 'polygraph/Hill'.

81

In the offices of the New York Times, a clerk was opening the mail and sorting it to different departments when he noticed an envelope with the lettering "The Emperor of Earth" instead of stamps.

Inside were a personal columns advertisement, and an imperial note to cover the cost.

The message was simple.

"The Emperor desires to contract with nations for the following classes of services:

"Burial of nuclear, biological or chemical hazardous wastes five to ten miles below the surface.

"Controlled pressure relief of active volcanoes.

"Placement of icebergs in desert locations.

"Other large scale engineering projects of national import.

"Send Lat/Long and time (flexible) with proposal to one of the following venues:"

After that followed a list of a dozen international newspapers that had 'Letters to the Emperor' columns and another dozen web sites who maintained open newsgroup services.

82

"So there's no way to turn it off or on?" asked Mr. Harrison.

Archer shook his head, "No. Zero maintenance. Just drive your trucks through this one, and back through the other one."

The head of the trucking company was an executive now, but he had the looks of one who'd come up the ranks driving his own rig. He smoked his cigar in short rapid puffs and scowled at the two hangars in the open parking area. There was a cool breeze coming off Lake Michigan, and Archer tried not to stick his hands in his pockets.

"It's safe? I don't want my drivers going through anything unsafe."

"Quite safe. How would you like to take a stroll with me?" He gestured toward the opening and took the first step.

The two men walked into the large open building.

"Keep to the side and use the hand rail," said Archer. There was a breeze to his back. He waited until Mr. Harrison came up behind him and grabbed onto the railing.

"The bridge looks scarier than it is. It will seem to twist under you when you take the first step."

In front of them, the metal walkway appeared to drop down below ground level and it seemed curved to such a steep grade that no one could keep their feet under them.

Archer stepped through the surface of the sphere, and his 'down' shifted. The walkway now appeared to go up. He stepped two paces and let go of the handrail and waved encouragingly to Harrison.

The trucker executive clamped his cigar in his teeth and followed. "Whoa."

"A little dizzying the first time, isn't it? But we're past the hard part. Just walk over this bridge and another twist at the end. It should be easier for your truckers, fastened in with their seatbelts."

They walked the arching bridge, wide enough for a big-rig truck with an oversized load, and then made their exits on the other side.

Archer smiled as he stepped back onto level ground in the wet humid, salt air. Harriman followed confidently.

Mr. Yakama bowed in greeting. Archer made the introductions and as the two businessmen exchanged their formal greetings, he gazed across the water to where Mt. Fuji was barely visible in the distant haze.

The weather in Japan is nicer today.

Hundreds of ships were visible. How many of them would be out of business by this time next year? Harriman and Yakama would win and others just like them would go out of business. It was inevitable. Who could afford to load the modular shipping containers onto freighters and wait weeks for them to cross the Pacific Ocean, when you could drive the trucks there directly?

83

The federal office building was intimidating. There was even a metal detector at the entrance, and his mother was rattled as she had to dig through her purse to locate the comb that set off the alert.

The FBI men were polite but unsmiling as they went into the interview room. Diana and James sat across a plain wood table and after being offered doughnuts and coffee, the questions started.

For the most part, they were the same ones from before. But after thirty minutes or so, they were all variations on one theme.

"Where is Robert now?"

Diana Hill had lost patience with the officers. She tried to be polite, but it was an uphill battle.

"I don't know. I left a message on his voicemail, but we never know when he will be in cell phone range to notice it. I gave you the number. Call him yourself."

"And you think he is in Seattle?"

"Yes. That's where he has been for weeks now."

"How do you know?"

Diana tried to be calm and just answer the questions. There was nothing to worry about.

"We take him to the airport and that's where he goes."

"Have you seen him get on the plane?"

"No. Where have you been lately? No one but the ticketed fliers can go up to the gates these days. I drop him off at the ticketing entrance."

"Have you seen the tickets?"

"No. He uses the Internet and has a confirmation number."

"Then how do you know he is going to Seattle."

"Because my husband told me so."

"And you believe him?"

"Yes. If you knew him, you would know he is a decent, honest man. He wouldn't lie to me."

The agent nodded and looked again at his notepad. He sighed.

"Mrs. Hill. We have checked with every airline that leaves here. None of them have any record of flights for a Robert Hill. Do you have any reason to suspect that he would be traveling under an assumed name?"

Diana was shocked silent.

The agent turned to James. "You say that you took your father to the airport one time? What did you observe?"

James shrugged. "We said goodbye, he took his suitcase into the airport and I drove off."

"He said he was going to Seattle?"

"I don't recall. That's where his job was. I don't usually question him about his jobs."

"You don't usually question him? But you have at some time?"

"Well, yes. I asked him to take me along. I could help him with little jobs—be a go-fer."

"What did he say?"

"He said no. He said there were security restrictions, and there wasn't anything more he could tell me."

The agent closed his notebook.

"Well, I'm not sure what more we can do here. If you would agree to a little test to confirm what you have already told us, I'm sure that that will be all."

Diana asked, "A test? What kind of test?"

"A polygraph test. We have the instrument here and we could take care of it right away, and be out of your hair."

"Oh." She seemed nervous. "I guess it would be okay."

The agent smiled. "And you, James?"

"No. No way in the world."

Both his mother and the agent seemed surprised. "Why not?"

"I don't trust you."

The agent seemed to consider that and then turned to Diana. "Okay, we can get your test and then you can tell James what it is like. Maybe he won't be afraid then."

She was led away by another agent.

"James, what are your concerns about the polygraph? It is a safe, simple procedure. Are you afraid of the electricity?"

"No."

"What is it then? Do you have something to hide?"

James laughed bitterly. He had practiced this speech. "Of course! You know the law better than I do. How many laws have you broken today? A dozen? I'm not a Catholic and I don't believe in original sin, but with all the laws on the books today a baby can hardly be born today without accidentally becoming a criminal.

"But that's not even the real reason. For some reason, my father is being caught up in some kind of witch-hunt. The worst thing I could do right now is let some statement of mine be distorted into evidence against him.

"My father is honest. Do you know how many times I have seen him correct a store clerk who has undercharged him?

"Do you know that in my whole life, I caught him lying only one time. Only one time! My cousins and my aunt and uncle and the rest of us went to the lake to try out our new boat. We were touring around the lake and the lake patrol stopped to check on our life jackets. The patrolman asked about the temporary boat license and my father claimed the boat was a week newer than it really was.

"That was it. It is such a vivid memory in my mind because my father is so scrupulously honest. Whatever crime you think he is guilty of, you must be wrong."

"Then take the polygraph test and convince us."

"No. Don't you realize I'm a teenager? I've been on the Internet all my life. I know exactly how polygraphy works. I know the questions, how you feed lies to the subject, how you calibrate the meters.

"A polygraph is just a machine to test galvanic responses. It's the operator and the procedure that are rife with dishonesty. Any subject that knows the tricks can defeat the readings. And any operator can 'prove' anyone guilty or innocent on a whim. Polygraphy is a sham and anyone with any sense should never take one.

"There's a reason polygraphy is invalid as court evidence, and there's a reason every major CIA spy scandal had the spy breezing through their polygraph screenings.

"The lie-detector is just a big lie.

"I'm not going to step into the lion's mouth and pray that he's not hungry!"

They asked again, several times, but James stonewalled.

I'm lying, and no matter what they say, no matter what it looks like, I can't risk a lie detector.

His speech had been part truth, part quotes from an anti-polygraph web site, and part outright lies.

The story of his father on the boat had been true, he had only seen his father lie once, up until he had been laid-off.

It's this secrecy that does it. What he said at the beginning—'this is a secret, and I can't tell you'—at least that had been honest.

But James couldn't take that line with the FBI. They beat you down, they were relentless, the followed up on every slip of the tongue.

Which was more damaging? The truth or a lie?

84

Rudy Ghest gave his report. The Interpol presence inside the FBI was being tolerated but he knew that would last only as long as he was being useful.

"That makes three nations that're ready to negotiate with the Emperor. At least, that's the number that are obviously represented in the newspaper columns. There could be others that are trying to contact him through more obscure methods."

The man with no badge asked, "Do your people have any influence to stop them?"

"Do I have any influence to stop the US from doing anything? No. The State Department will have to do that on their own."

Who is this guy? Rudy had asked Jay, but he didn't know either.

"Don't they realize what a mistake it is to give official recognition to this criminal?"

"He has offered some considerable prizes. The French newspapers are making noises that a deep rock nuclear repository would be a smart move. Even in the US people are saying that, I hear."

"Oh, yes, his offers sound good on the surface, but you have to remember his claimed one billion a year tax. Recognize his legitimacy and you could be bound to pay up.

"But that's just looking at the good side. Take a look at his list.

"If he can move CBR wastes to deep under the earth, he could just as easily move them anywhere! How about dumping Hanford nuclear wastes on New York City or Washington DC?

"And the volcano thing—how about spreading a pyroclastic flow over Chicago?

"Or dropping an iceberg across the Mississippi River at St. Louis? It would flood out the whole Corn Belt before it broke, and then the whole path to the Gulf would be scoured clean.

"We have a disaster any way you look at it. And there is one rogue crazy with his finger on the trigger."

Rudy remembered a conference less than a year ago, just before he had signed on to Interpol, when a French agent had ranted in just the same way about the American President. There was always something fearful about one man exercising horrific powers—even though that was the whole of history. Parliaments and legislatures never gave the orders; it always boiled down to one man.

CBR, Rudy thought to himself, *That's the old name for NBC, nuclear-biological-chemical hazards. How many years had 'NoBadge' been at this?*

The other taskforce reports were interesting.

Discrete monitoring of everyone who had offered to work for the Emperor was showing promise. They had detected significant lifestyle changes in over a dozen. Court-ordered bugging of some of them had begun.

Several groups had begun significant commercial use of teleportation without informing the FBI. No action had been taken to shut them down, although the legal arguments were being prepared. More surveillance was ordered.

A wide net had been cast for suspects, using such vague clues as the phrasing of the original UN announcement. That was now starting to show up potential candidates.

Of the dozen or so suspects, one was mentioned in particular—an out-of-work physicist who had taken a secretive job in Seattle, but who apparently had vanished. His family was being monitored.

85

Bob set the pallet of paper down with a crunch, as the teleportation dropped it an inch or two above the gravel. He closed the portal and walked over to his printer.

That ought to keep me in imperials for another few months.

His initial estimates had been off. But it had been an honest mistake. If he'd only bought his goods and services with big bills, it wouldn't have taken so much paper to print them. But when he realized that it was important to have people trade the imperials themselves, in order to establish it as a real currency, then more smaller bills were needed.

Not too many people would bid for a fifty-thousand imperial note, but there would be a brisk trade in fifty's, even if there were a thousand of them.

He cut the top off the first box and picked up a ream of paper. This style of paper had been hard to find. It wasn't all that special, but once he started with it, he had to keep using it. There were already counterfeit imperials in circulation, and paper style was one of the clues people used to determine the real from the fake.

One of these days, I'll need to issue a new version. Maybe on the anniversary of the empire, or maybe when I can gain recognition. But people will have to know it's coming. He hadn't had time to come up with a design that really pleased him.

A button-press opened the hopper on the printer. He popped open the wrapping paper on the ream and held it over the tray.

Inside his chest, his heart started hammering like a machinegun.

Oh, no!

86

That's a different car tailing me.

James noted the color and make. He'd started writing them down. If he could cross-check them against the names of the agents he'd already listed, perhaps it would give him an edge later.

His after-hours spying had located the complete FBI file on his family.

Dad made such a tiny mistake. When he composed the foreign language greetings in his UN announcement, he had bought several language practice CD's and copied the greetings word for word. When some obsessive-compulsive in the FBI analyzed them, he had been able to flag the specific language courses. A search of all bookstores had led them to Robert Hill's credit card.

James would love to be able to delete the offending FBI report, but it'd spread far and wide. That was what he had to do now, follow the chain of reports, from the local office to the Dallas Office, up to some task force. At each level, he was finding critical agents, and marking wristwatches.

If they decided to move on his father, or on them, he had to be ready.

James no longer had any doubts. His father had to be the Emperor. He was hiring help at various levels, according to the FBI, but except for the elusive Archer, it seemed that none of them actually teleported.

I've got to contact Dad. Somehow.

There was no mention of bugging the house in the FBI reports, but would they mention it before they did it?

I need to wipe the computer, make sure they can't get at Dad through me.

Maybe I should erase all command functions from my watch too.

But once I do that, I lose the ability to watch the FBI.

And he would never see Oriel again.

I wish I had a Tempest system. Supposedly that secure computer system was proof against indirect monitoring.

With ordinary computers, stray radio waves made by the scanning dot on normal computer screens, or even the flicker of a keyboard, could be picked up at a distance and reconstructed with sophisticated equipment. *The FBI could be reading my screen without even bugging the place.*

He got up again and went to the front porch. One advantage to living out in the country was that he could hear every car for a mile around. What was the range on that spy system?

I'm probably safe for tonight. Then I'll shut it down.

But why didn't he make one last sweep? Tell Oriel why he was going away. Find his father and alert him to the FBI. Then he could return home, shut everything down, and pretend to be innocent until his father could figure it all out.

He pulled up the screen. This was going to be the last time he could reprogram his watch functions.

The software had changed again. Daddy's been busy.

He reviewed the new functions.

Oh, I like this.

87

Ngarta looked again at the sun. The food package was definitely late. Regular as clockwork, it had been. And now it was late. Was his warden trying to starve him now? Well, there were fish.

But what about the water? If he cut off the water he would die.

Ngarta sprang to his feet and started sprinting towards the creek. Water was still flowing, but he had to see for himself if the source was still falling from the sky.

88

"Sir. You wished to be notified. The Emperor has missed a pickup."

"Details?" Admiral Forsythe asked.

"An imperial agent, one we didn't even know about, reported that an expected contact didn't go off. It was a telephone report, and she is too frightened to come in. She's testing the waters for amnesty."

"Pull her in. Talk to our other informants. If we can get confirmation, then our trap has sprung. Call Heisman. Be ready to strike."

89

James removed Grumpy's hard disk and put it in his pocket. It balanced the weight of the drive in his other pocket. He had gutted his bedroom computer shortly after typing 'Bail'. An old software advertisement had come to plague his imagination. It had claimed sophisticated methods could retrieve even erased files. He didn't have the software to protect the data, so he would have to dispose of the hard drives themselves.

The gutted computers would be incriminating, but if the FBI got close enough to open up his computers, then the game was over anyway. He wasn't trying to avoid giving them evidence for a trial. He was trying to protect his father.

He replaced the computer's case and put an auto-boot CD in the drive. A casual check wouldn't even notice the machine had no hard-drive.

Okay, that's it. All I've got is my watch.

And it was loaded. He had put a dozen locations in the normal list. **LIGHT** was programmed to step through the locations—he no longer had to go through the whole merry-go-round to get to the place where he wanted to go. Of course he had to keep the list in his head. Memorizing it had been hard.

And **START** turned on 'SevenLeagueBoots'. He had taken a quick look at the code and he was dying to try it out.

No time like the present.

It was broad daylight out. His mother was off at work, in spite of the fact her nerves were shot. Just over the hill, he knew that an FBI agent had parked beside the road and had a telescope trained at their property.

He walked over to the hidden side of the house.

START

He looked carefully. Supposedly he was surrounded by two concentric spheres, but he couldn't see them.

He took a small step. Nothing happened.

He took a bigger one, and abruptly, he was twenty feet away. *Good.*

In an explosive burst, like blasting off the starting blocks in a race, he took off running.

The scenery around him flickered with each pace. Only the sky looked stable, except for the clouds.

He dropped out of the run, slowing until he flickered to a stop.

Where am I?

He was in a pine forest. There were no pine forests within a hundred miles of his house.

I had been facing north. There are trees like this near Dallas. I ran to Dallas? He giggled.

"Cut that out." He told himself. "You've got hard-drives to dispose of."

He looked at the sky and started trotting towards the east. He settled into an easy pace, watching the landscape flicker past him. *It's like the Flash, in the comic books! Only I don't have to watch out for obstacles.*

From the glimmerings he had of the software, every time his foot moved out of the inner sphere into the outer one, the code calculated how fast his foot was moving and in what direction. He was teleported in the appropriate direction at a distance calculated from the rate he was running.

Of course, each time the sphere appeared, the full gamut of safety features were in play. He wouldn't run into anything, and he would always appear on solid ground.

This is fun.

Abruptly, his eye caught a glint of sunlight off a glass pyramid.

Memphis? Memphis, Tennessee. And that must be the Mississippi River.

He turned south and paced the river for a few dozen miles. *Good enough.* Dropping to a walk, he edged close to the muddy banks and tossed in the hard disks.

Nothing around but a couple of farm houses.

He started running again, following the curving river, trying to keep close. Sometimes he would misstep and end up on the opposite shore as the software kept him from stepping into the water.

The riverside was getting more and more industrialized.

I should stop. But the running was addictive.

New Orleans? The city blossomed all around him and then faded away. He began to slow. *I'll run into the Gulf of Mexico.*

He dropped to a walk. And stopped.

All around him were buildings. He saw a sign.

That's Spanish. Where am I?

A car puttered down the street. It was an ancient Chevy. *It's held together with wire and spit.*

Parked beside the road was an old Ford pickup, looking equally well preserved.

"Hello?" he asked the man resting in the pickup. "What is the name of this town?"

"*¿Qué?*"

James pointed to the ground. "This town, this city. What is its name?"

The man nodded, understanding. "Habana."

Oops. Havana, Cuba. I must have stepped across the Gulf of Mexico by accident. Which way is north?

He looked around, but the streets were curved and twisted. He should have been paying attention to the sun.

Or why even go back north? I could go east, step across the Atlantic?

But no, without a map he would get even more lost.

He pressed **START**. *No more seven league boots without at least a compass.*

LIGHT LIGHT ADJUST.

He stumbled to his knees.

Dark again. I must be in Paris.

He was just outside her apartment building. A couple on the street were looking at him strangely.

James got to his feet and walked out of sight. When they passed, he went back to her apartment.

He knocked lightly on her door. Oriel opened it instantly, and pulled him inside.

"Where have you been? I was so worried."

He returned her hug. "Problems with the USA FBI. My house is no longer safe."

"They're coming for you too?"

"What do you mean?"

She waved to the television. CNN was showing police in riot gear dragging people from their houses.

"The police aren't saying, but the reporters say that these are agents of the Emperor."

James felt a chill. Things were happening too fast.

"Oriel, I have been interrogated by the police and thus far, they haven't arrested me. However, I might have to go into hiding, or at least pretend to be perfectly normal for a while. I wanted you to know why I went away."

"Can you take me with you?"

He smiled. "I don't want to go away, but there is no place I could hide you, not with the police watching my every move."

He glanced at the TV screen. "And now might not be the best time to become an agent of the Emperor."

"I don't care. No one can stop the Emperor! He will do something, I am sure. Don't you lose faith. Don't leave me behind."

He nodded. He wanted to tell her more, but the more she knew, the more dangerous it would be for her, and the more danger she could be for his father.

He took her wrist.

"You bought this watch recently." She nodded.

"The Emperor has the ability to program new features into it. Think of it as a remote control. I don't have authorization to give you teleport access, but I did add something to your watch."

He showed her how to press the buttons in a certain pattern to activate it.

"And now, my watch and your watch are connected.

"Look here." He picked up a pencil from her table. Carefully he pushed it towards her watch, and as it entered a tiny sphere, barely visible that floated a centimeter above the watch face, the tip poked out of the same sphere near his watch.

Her eyes were locked on the sight. Her mouth was open.

"See, how the angle of the pencil stays the same, no matter which direction I hold the watch?"

She nodded. "What do I do with it?"

"It is a channel between us. It is just like a hole through space connecting us. We can talk through it. You can look through it. If you need to talk to me, open this sphere and listen very carefully, to make sure that I am not being questioned by the police. If everything looks safe, then make a small noise, or tap the crystal of my watch—something very small to get my attention. If I respond, then we can talk.

"We will have to be very careful. Can you do this for me?"

"I will do anything."

90

James appeared in the darkened gallery of computers.

Warning buzzers, of several kinds, were filling the air with whoops and sweeps and raspberries.

"Dad! Dad, it's me, James!" He called out. Time for secrecy was over. He needed to confess all and let his father know what was going on.

But why all the alarms? He started walking around the place. The alarms were enough to drive him crazy.

What was going on?

No one was there. Had the FBI gotten his father too?

He went to a computer terminal. The sphere software was already up.

Check the logs. That would give him a hint where his father was.

But the log files were jumbled. Dots and feathers flickered all over the screen when he tried to read them.

Dad encrypted them. It was the only thing that made sense. Why would he do that?

The alarms bored into his head. He would have to stop them, before he could think.

It wasn't a power failure, or hardware, apparently.

Status. He clicked the icon. A wide window opened up with numerous blinking boxes.

He clicked on one.

"Dropbox 34: Heat alarm. Chemical alarm." There was a whole string of options to check. Mute alarm was one. He clicked it. Maybe one of the voices of the alarm chorus stopped, but he couldn't be sure.

He went to the next. It was very similar. He stopped its alarm too.

The third was a voice message from Agent 1:

"This is Archer. Four or more police were waiting for me at FedEx headquarters. I don't know whether they turned me in or not, but I just barely missed getting vaccinated with a dart gun. They didn't even call out. Shoot first, I guess. I'll be hiding out you-know-where until I hear from you."

James paused. *I could fight this screen all day.*

Is Mom in trouble? The question popped into his head with compelling force.

He switched to the familiar sphere control screen, located the 'Home' location and looked.

FBI cars were parked in the driveway. He flew the tiny monitor camera through the house. No sign of her. Was she still at work?

He flew it up and towards town.

There! That's her store. He approached, and then stopped when he saw the flashing lights by the entrance.

Mom! She was being led to a police car in handcuffs.

Damage Control

91

James had the full power of the teleportation system at his fingertips, and he was very angry.

A dozen plans flashed through his mind.

Killing people won't help anything.

The police car started to move.

Does she have a wristwatch? He didn't know. He had never thought about it.

He followed the car. It was the only thing he could do until they stopped. Plucking her out of the car would only throw her against the wall with whatever speed the car was moving.

But he had to be ready. He picked a safe location, set up the transfer. All he had to do was wait.

The police car pulled to a stop at a red light.

James clicked the button.

Then pressed another.

"Oof!" Diana Hill cried as she dropped six inches into the church pew.

James appeared out of nowhere beside her.

"Are you okay Mom?" He was beside her.

"James? Oh, James!" She reached for him, but the handcuffs were in the way. He put his arms around her.

"It was horrible. Right there in front of Ruth and my boss, they just came and took me, in handcuffs. I'll never be able to face them again."

"It's okay Mom. They don't have you anymore."

"James," she had a frantic, panicked look in her eyes. "James, what is going on?"

"Mom, Daddy is the Emperor."

She paled. "So it is true. Why didn't he tell me?" There were tears in her eyes.

"He didn't tell me either." That didn't seem to make it any better.

James continued, "I found out by accident, when I was playing with his computer."

She looked very angry, but she wasn't looking at him. "Why? Why did he do this?"

"I don't know. I can only guess that he had a good reason for becoming the Emperor, but I do know why he didn't tell us."

"Why?" she snapped.

"Because that made us innocent bystanders, instead of accomplices. Keeping you in the dark let you pass their lie-detector test with flying colors. My snooping meant I couldn't risk it."

She shook her head, "Not good enough. He lied to me!"

James glanced around the church auditorium. No one was there, but if she was much louder, people in the offices could hear. He had no idea what his mother wanted to do. At least here, she would be certain to have friends with her. Perhaps even someone who would hide her from the police.

"You are mad at him?" He asked.

She nodded. Tears were streaming down her face and she couldn't seem to make words come out.

James gave her a hug. She hugged back, and then gripped his shoulder. "You didn't tell me either."

"I couldn't. It wouldn't have been safe."

"You men!" He couldn't tell if she was angry with him or not. "Couldn't you just ask me if I wanted to be protected from all this?"

She paused. "Did Bob invent this teleportation?"

James shrugged. "I guess he did. I never could figure out what he was doing in the work shed."

"Me neither."

"Mom?"

"Yes?"

"I don't think he expected to survive this."

"What do you mean?"

Just then, he saw a reflection through the rear windows. Someone was coming to check them out. Church had been the safest place to bring her, but adding another person to the dragnet of Emperor sympathizers didn't seem smart right now.

"We're out of time. The police are arresting everyone who has anything to do with the Emperor. I saw it on the news. You can come with me, or stay here."

"Go where?"

"To the Emperor's base."

Her eyes tightened, "You know how to go there?"

"Yes."

Just then, the auditorium door opened. "Is anybody in here?" called the church secretary.

"I'm going. What do I do?" Diana whispered.

"Hug me tight."

92

The Emperor Task Force meeting was something different this time. The place was like a war room. Rudy Ghest had nothing to do but stay out of people's way as the FBI scurried all around him, taking phone messages and filling in squares on a big whiteboard. Supposedly, it detailed all known agents of the Emperor.

Messages were coming from the UK, Germany and possibly other countries as well, but not through Interpol channels. This crackdown was being orchestrated at a different level altogether.

Someone had ordered an attack on the Empire. No one was claiming victory, although from the excited whispers and glances he could see, things must be going well for them.

NoBadge had come striding through the place like he owned it, and then left shortly thereafter.

It was very puzzling. What kind of an attack could possibly work against an opponent who could be anywhere, and who could pull your captives out of jail instantly?

But that wasn't what he was hearing. People were being arrested, and jailed. And they weren't evaporating away.

93

"What do you mean, missing?" Diana Hill was shouting to be heard over the alarms.

James spread his hands wide. "I don't know. This is his base. All his computers are here. That monitor right over there has the control software. Daddy even listed this location as 'Base'.

"But he isn't here. His stuff is out of control, and screeching like demons to catch his attention.

"Something is wrong. I have to find him."

She looked at the computers. All this was the work of her husband? Where were they?

She tried to put her hands to her ears. "What can I do to help?"

James said, "Stand still. I need to get your handcuffs off first." He opened a new sphere about two feet in diameter from the computer controls.

"Wave your arms through it." She did, and nothing happened. "Do it again," he said. This time the handcuffs fell to the floor under the other sphere.

James waved her over to the computer screen. Step by step, he showed her how to turn off the alarms.

"Go down this list. Open each box and turn off each alarm. Don't do anything else. Not yet."

She nodded. Hesitantly, she moved the mouse pointer to the first item on the list.

He moved over to another computer and started hunting.

The encrypted logs could tell him a lot, if only he could decrypt them.

He tried the two passwords he knew his father had used in the past, but with no luck.

Later. Guessing passwords to could take forever.

He glanced at his watch, then grinned.

The location database had grown huge. His father had even added a search function. Typing in 'watch' produced a list of over 300 entries. He scanned down, and then clicked on 'My Watch'.

The info window listed the type. He was right. It was exactly the same type of watch he'd bought his father.

He created a search window on 'My Watch'. There was hardly any light. Carefully, he moved the viewpoint away from the watch.

This is wrong. He's not wearing it.

The watch was lying on gravel.

He started a slow spiral search around the watch, looking and listening.

It was the sound that clued him in.

His mother was gradually eliminating the alarms, but the watch was making alarm sounds as well. Like an echo, a fraction of a second later.

He raised the viewpoint and panned the camera.

There!

He got up from his chair and sprinted off among the racks of computers.

The watch was lying on the ground, next to a computer. He picked it up.

The light was still dim, but he could make out the mess.

Scattered across the gravel was a spilled ream of paper, and next to his feet was a shallow pit in the gravel, like a sphere had swallowed what was on the ground, along with the gravel underneath.

He eyeballed the scene for a minute or two, trying to put the pieces together.

It was the printer that finally added the last clue.

Here was where his father printed his imperial notes. He had picked up a ream of paper to load the printer. Something had happened then. He dropped the ream, spilling it, and then falling to the ground.

He then tossed his wristwatch over against the computer as a sphere swallowed him away.

"Mother! Come over here."

He heard her approach, and he stopped her.

"See that paper. Don't get anywhere near it. It's poisoned."

"What?"

"Someone slipped Daddy a ream of paper laced with a contact poison. It knocked him down and then he vanished. Without him handling all the teleport systems, it started malfunctioning."

"But where is he?" She sounded distraught.

He shook his head. "I don't know, but I know where to look."

94

Rudy listened to the reports.

"It was nearly a clean sweep. Once we saw that the Emperor's teleport system had stopped, we were able to move in and capture the agents. They are all being interrogated now." He wasn't an FBI agent. In his black suit he looked like a junior version of NoBadge.

Rudy asked, "Has the Emperor been captured?"

"Not as yet, but our information suggests that if he is not already dead, he will be captured soon."

"What information is this?"

The agent shook his head. "That information is classified. All I am allowed to say is that action by the United States has removed the international terrorist threat who called himself the 'Emperor'."

Rudy had expected as much. "What about Archer?"

"Unfortunately, he was able to elude the force that was assigned to him, but since we have his photo and details about the man, we expect ordinary police work to turn him up shortly. And besides, without the teleportation system, he is no threat."

Rudy nodded. "I have enough for my report."

The man smiled. "I should think so."

Rudy didn't have the heart to tell him what his report would be. They had rounded up all the new agents, agents that had only hired on with the Emperor after he had already demonstrated his ability to steal anything anywhere. Without the Emperor, or his teleporter machine, they had nothing.

95

Admiral Forsythe stared at the map on his office wall, thinking.

Unless I can produce his body, it will never be over. Many of the teleportation stations are still running strong—the oil pipeline, the water shipments, even that trucking facility. Only the Emperor knows how to shut them down. The best we can do is quarantine them.

Unless we can control them, they are just a disaster waiting to happen.

A light appeared on his phone. He picked it up.

"The paper supply has been loaded into the truck."

"Any accidents."

"None, sir."

"Get it all to the secure incinerator. I want no fallout from this."

"Understood, sir."

At least one thing had worked to plan.

The Emperor had been printing his own money, which meant supplies from the outside. He'd stocked up on ink at the very beginning, but he had underestimated his supply of that textured paper.

We withdrew it all from circulation, except for a small stash at the factory. Our stash.

96

Mayor Bill Norris walked along the top of the Big Lake dam. He had seen the news reports. People were saying that the Emperor was dead. He didn't know what to think about that. His deal with the devil seemed to have paid off. The lake was nearly full now, just an inch or so from the spillway. It had cost the city, but the fishing trade was booming, especially since it had been discovered that the lake now contained black grayling, whitefish, and a kind of salmon which were supposed to only be available in Siberian lakes. Every morning, a new batch of fishing boats headed out for the cold spot, where the fishing was best.

It was good water too, clear and pure.

He stepped down onto the spillway and walked to the edge. The water was still coming up. He made his last payment, but the Emperor hadn't picked it up. Nor the note he had left thanking him for the water and requesting that the transfer stop now.

If he's dead, what happens now? The creek bed has been dry for a long time now. I guess that's about to change.

97

"James, what do we do now?" his mother asked.

He was deep into the programming of his father's watch. It had only four buttons, like his did, but his father had layered functions on top of escape patterns, on top of menus. Considering there was no feedback to tell you where you were, that you would have to hold it all in your head, he was impressed. The watch was totally useless as a timekeeper. Trying to set it would likely trigger a landslide in Albania or something.

Why did he throw it away when the poison hit?

"James?"

"Sorry Mom. I'm trying to understand this. What did you want?"

She put her hand on his shoulder. "I stopped the alarms."

He raised his head and listened. The deep rock gallery was now quiet. Spooky quiet, with the only sounds being the low murmur of computer fans.

"Good work."

"But what do we do now. A lot of those signals were serious."

"Show me."

They stepped over to her screen.

Most of the status icons were still blinking. James checked the settings and sorted them by priority. He clicked the first one.

"Drop box 9: Overpressure, overtemperature. Camera disabled."

There was an info box. He clicked it, but it showed an error: Log file unreadable.

A half-dozen of the drop boxes were like that. James chose one and carefully established a pinhole-sized portal connecting between the drop box, which was apparently nearby and somewhere over the Pacific Ocean.

The pressure started to drop, and then the temperature flared higher and the pressure climbed again. James widened the leak hole and it was soon stable. When the pressure had dropped to normal, he moved a viewpoint inside the dropbox.

It was just a pile of ashes. Papers of some kind.

James jumped up and walked back over to where the printer sat, and the ground was covered with the poisoned papers. There sat a stack of paper reams, still wrapped in their brightly colored advertisements, still piled neatly on the shipping pallet.

So his father didn't have time to dispose of the other poisoned papers. So what did he burn?

The more he thought of it, the more he was reminded of the 'Bail' program back on the home computer—an automated procedure to destroy all the evidence in an emergency.

"What is it James?"

"Dad did something. When he felt himself getting sick, he started a program, probably from his watch, that burned some critical notes, then it transported him somewhere, and then encrypted the logs of that transfer."

He looked at his mother, straight in her eyes. "He didn't expect to survive. He knew being the Emperor was dangerous and that somehow, some enemy would get to him. He was ready.

He had it all planned out. One command from his wristwatch and he could secure the base and transport himself someplace."

"But where?"

James nodded, "Some place safe, is what I would guess. A hospital? Poison is about the only way they could sneak in here.

"Dad didn't know anyone had the keys to this place but him, and he was the only one who brought things in. That's why he had those 'drop boxes'—places where money and stuff could be safely transferred while he tested to see if it was what it was supposed to be.

"I'd bet this wasn't the first poison attempt."

Diana Hill was taking it in, but it was a lot to absorb. "A hospital. But which one."

James looked at her. She was holding up pretty well. It had been years since he thought his mother was infallible and capable of handling everything, but maybe she was stronger than he'd thought.

"Can you handle the status board while I keep hunting through the programs?"

She shook her head. "I can do word processing and spreadsheets and balance my checkbook, but I don't understand what all these windows do. You could show me, but you need to be hunting for Bob."

He nodded. "I do know someone who can help."

98

"Any luck with the hospitals?" Admiral Forsythe asked.

"Not yet. It might be quicker if we sent out a notice to be on the lookout for him." The man in the black suit stood at attention while he talked.

"No. People are watching us closely. If we sent out a description of the symptoms, that would be bad politically. We have pictures of our top suspects, but still, letting it be known what they look like is not wise.

"Even if he's dead, I want the body, not anyone else."

99

CNN Top Headlines:

Typhoon Koppu is approaching Japan after devastating Okinawa.

President Rizal of the Philippines sends troops to quell riot in capital.

Emperor believed still missing—US Marshall's office quarantining teleportation sites.

100

Oriel appeared in a bubble that blinked into existence, and then vanished. James was there to catch her.

"*C'était intense!*"

"Are you okay?" he asked as he helped her to her feet. "I warned you about that first step."

Oriel noticed Diana, and glanced at James.

He smiled, "Oriel, this is Diana, the Empress of Earth."

Oriel bowed, "Greetings, your Majesty."

Diana smiled, glancing at the young French girl, and her son. "*Vous êtes très bienvenu. Nous n'avons pas établi des protocoles encore, ainsi oubliez le cintrage. Appelez-moi Diana.*"

James mouth dropped open. "I didn't know you spoke French." To Oriel, he said, "Parents! They are always surprising you."

Oriel blinked. "She is your mother? That makes you...."

He nodded, "Sorry. Yes, I guess that makes me Crown Prince James. Sounds silly, I know."

She took a deep breath. Things were happening quickly. "You said I was needed."

James took her by the hand, instantly grave, "Yes. My father is missing, and I need you to help my mother control the operation."

"Me?"

"Yes. You know there are other agents, but none of them, without exception—not even me, were trained on the daily operation of the teleporters. When the Emperor was poisoned, and went missing, many of the regular tasks were stalled, waiting for someone to make the right decision.

"My mother, in spite of her many other admirable skills, is not computer talented, as I know you are. You can be a big help. Come over here."

He sat them down before the screen. An alarm went off.

"Mother, show Oriel how to silence that."

Cautiously, Diana moved the mouse, opened the window. She clicked the alarm off.

"Now see what caused it."

When Diana paused, Oriel pointed at the info panel.

"Carbon Dioxide levels elevated in Base."

James caught himself breathing. It was true, the air in here was stale.

He said, "Now, figure out what to do."

Diana said, "I would open a window, but there aren't any windows are there?"

Oriel fearlessly clicked the options. "Here is one—external portal."

She looked at James questioningly.

"Ask my mom. You two will have to make these kinds of decisions."

The women looked at each other and shrugged. "I guess so," said Diana.

Oriel nodded and activated that option. A second panel opened up, showing a dozen locations, and a timer.

"Mid-Pacific? Ten minutes?"

She activated it.

Suddenly, the light in the gallery brightened as sunlight streamed into the cave through a large hole. They all got to their feet and walked closer.

"I can smell the salt air."

"And the moisture."

James said, "Listen, you can hear the wind." The air was no longer stuffy.

"It worked," said his mother.

"He must have pre-set a lot of the options. Notice how it didn't open over any of the equipment. If it happened to be raining, he would have a chance to close it before too much water came in. Too much moisture will be bad for the computers."

Oriel nodded, "Next time, we'll use the desert location."

They waited until the window to the Pacific vanished, and then they went back to the computer screen.

James pointed over to the other screen. "I've got to get back to my search. You two will need to review all of the status alerts. If a decision is easy, then do it. If it is hard, then think it through, but still do it. You can come bother me, but it will slow down my hunt for my father. Can you do it?"

They nodded and sat down to work.

Diana watched James head off to his computer screen. She had to trust that her son knew what he was doing. Bob's life was probably in his hands. He seemed to be taking the responsibility like a man.

"Diana?" Oriel hesitated over the name, "Do you wish to start here, or look at the older ones?"

"The older ones, I guess.

"Tell me Oriel, when did you first meet my son?"

101

"Hey, Boss, the sluice is flowing again. I've started the pump."

Alex Lupin got up from his desk and unlocked the cabinet. "The payment is still there." Two thousand imperials still rested in a bundle wrapped with a blue rubber band.

Jeff laughed, "Well, don't touch it. I've got the boys working. There is definitely color there."

"Cross your fingers that it will last. I thought we were dead when we missed the last payment. Have you located more imperials?"

"I don't know. Ever since 'the Emperor is dead' rumors started, the price of imperials has been all over the map."

"Well keep looking. I still think running a gold mining operation without the mine is still a wonderful idea, but we have to keep our costs down. I would hate to pay for this in dollars."

Their operation looked like a simple warehouse, but they pumped in a mix of gold ore from an old placer deposit deep below the earth via teleportation, and then when the dregs settled, they were dumped back into the hole the same way.

No mess, no angry neighbors, no Environmental Protection Agency to watch over you. It was mining like Alex had always wanted.

Jeff rubbed his chin, "Boss, you know we were told to notify the feds if there was any more activity."

"I know, but you saw what the US Marshals did to Trans-Pacific trucking. A perfectly innocent business shut down. They'll do that to us as well. Tell the boys their paycheck depends on keeping quiet."

102

James hunted through the whole program database, looking for the 'crashandburn' program function. It was the only function programmed into his father's watch that he couldn't find the code for. Pressing **MODE** three times in quick succession should have started 'crashandburn', and he felt sure that is exactly what happened.

But his father had covered all his traces. The last thing the software routine had done, he was sure, was to delete itself.

At home, he would have checked the backups. His father was religious about backups. But here, with all the money in the world, he had mirrored everything instead. You could take a chainsaw to one of these Base computers and the load would magically be handled by its brothers. But deleting a file on this system deleted it everywhere.

Just then, there was a rumble. It seemed to come from everywhere.

Two female voices screamed in harmony.

"What's happened?" He was up out of his chair.

His mother looked pale.

Oriel waved at the screen. "We collected a report from a Los Angeles agent. I pushed the button, and there was an explosion."

"What was the command?"

"'Transfer to dropbox.'"

He kneeled down by the screen. He checked the log. Everything that had happened after 'crashandburn' was readable, if he scrolled past the encrypted part.

"An explosion all right. Someone substituted a bomb for the report. Probably the same people who arrested the agents. I knew the dropboxes were relatively close. But that sounded too close.

Oriel said, "We had already brought several payments into the dropboxes. Maybe we should stop."

"For now," he agreed. "Later we'll make it even safer. The only way our enemies can get to us is if we bring the weapon here ourselves, so let's don't do that."

103

A light came on in Admiral's Forsythe's on-site apartment. "Sir, we've located the Emperor's headquarters."

He was out of bed in an instant. "Show me."

Dressed in a robe, he followed his orderly to the situation room. On the wall a large computer display was rotating a 3-D map of a mountain. Below it, a large dot was blinking.

"Sir, this came from some data we got from the South Dakota School of Mines and Technology. Some months ago, researchers had noticed some unexplained seismic signals, but when they went away, the data was just shelved. Our queries brought it to mind and they forwarded it to us.

"This. This is new. Three hours ago, there was a single sharp signal from roughly the same location. And see here," he pointed to a line in the seismic image. "This is the edge of some kind of chamber."

"A cave?"

"No." The man tapped the map. "This is granite. No cave here."

The man in the bathrobe read the legend on the map, and then realized what he was looking at.

Bastard. Under some circumstances, he would have risked a tactical nuclear strike, even within the United States, to rid the world of this wild card.

But he couldn't nuke Mt. Rushmore.

104

Typhoon Koppu steered inland, lashing Yokohama and Tokyo with winds over a hundred miles per hour. The merchant fleet had several days warning, and a large fraction of them had moved down the coast towards Nagoya.

But on the shore, the buildings shook.

In the center of a large parking area, two new buildings creaked and groaned. They had been erected in a hurry, without the re-enforcement common in the typhoon plagued area.

The atmospheric pressure dropped steadily as the core of the storm approached. The windowless buildings began to bulge. All doors were locked, and sealed with chains. The air inside had to push hard to get out, but there was a lot of air inside. Each contained a large sphere that shared its interior with Chicago, currently experiencing a seasonal high pressure.

Sheet metal screws began to snap. The metal began to tear, and as a gust of wind from the storm stuck the buildings, they exploded, one a few seconds after the other.

The metal sides and girders were caught by the winds. Soon nothing was left.

Two spheres, slightly darker than the cloud-draped landscape, stood alone in the lot.

In Chicago, two other buildings stood draped with yellow police warning tape. The noise had brought police to investigate. One man made the mistake of opening a door, to investigate, and it was immediately ripped from its hinges. The man was blown off his feet, and was swallowed up like a dust bunny in a vacuum cleaner hose.

The wind howling through the opened doorway resonated like a steam-whistle. The entire building shook and the rest of the police retreated.

Ripping metal added to the noise as the metal building collapsed. Walls crumpled inward, and then the roof popped free of its crossbeams and imploded. Shortly the walls followed, vanishing into the sphere.

A vortex formed, with its point locked to the revealed sphere. The moisture-laden air from the lake condensed, revealing a strange sight—a waterspout dancing on land in bright sunlight, with not a cloud in the sky.

The vortex twisted and danced around the place like an angry snake. The police brought in re-enforcement to hold the crowd back.

Wild winds struck the neighboring building, and it was enough. The second one began collapsing, this time in front of a dozen filming news crews. As it vanished into its sphere, a second vortex formed. The brother winds danced and entangled, for an instant merging, and then breaking apart. Helicopters were warned back, the vortex gusts were reaching several hundred feet into the air.

In Japan, a Chicago policeman with a broken leg and a lacerated arm crawled slowly away from the howling blast of winds. A permanent explosion formed over the remains of two buildings.

105

Oriel called out, "James, come here."

He nodded, and typed the command to print the list he had just captured from a monitor screen. The printer began buzzing.

"Coming." He got up, and felt the aching muscles. He was stiff and starving. How long had he been at it?

"*Regardez ceci.*" She pointed at the television screen. Strange tornadoes were spinning slowly around each other in the middle of a city.

"I think that is one of ours," she said.

"What's going on?"

Diana said, "The commentator said it was a teleport gate between Chicago and Tokyo, designed for trucks to drive through. A typhoon hit Tokyo and it's sucking air through the gates. It's totally destroyed the facility, and a policeman has been sucked through.

"What do we do?"

"Was there any alarm?"

"Not that I can see. Bob didn't plan for that, I guess."

James scowled. An alarm would have the controls for those gates already identified. Now he would have to look for it.

"Is there any background? When was the gate created? The name of the company?"

He'd found the list of active portals before, but they weren't named, just a sequence of numbers. Portals were created and disposed of many times a day, and the computer kept track of it all. He started at the beginning, tapping the next key staccato, giving the status window just an instant to form the words before he went on to the next one.

Familiar names and locations flashed by, throwing him off his rhythm. The most common were watches.

How many watches does he have tagged? For each, there had to be an active portal. He had seen that code—a hundred watches shared a common radio detector. For a hundredth of a second, each would check its location against the persistent buzz of the watch's circuitry, before it was the next watch's time.

How many had he tagged? His own, Oriel's, a couple of dozen FBI men, and one Interpol guy.

There! Trans-Pacific Trucking Eastward Portal.

He opened the control panel and dialed it to zero diameter.

"James! One of them stopped."

Right. There were two of them. Then next click brought up the Westward Portal. He closed it as well.

"They're both stopped now."

James opened a monitor port to the Chicago location. Police were funneling in through the fenced gate. He zoomed his viewpoint over the mob. They looked like they were searching for something among the wreckage that hadn't been sucked through.

Oh yes, the missing policeman.

Oriel came up behind him. "What are you doing now?"

"Switching over to Japan. There's a man, maybe injured, out in that mess."

The screen showed near whiteout conditions as the storm winds were whipping rain sideways.

"Did the news report say which way he was sucked in?"

"No. Just that a door blew in and took him with it."

"I'll have to search a spiral, then. Do you know how to run one of these monitor screens?"

"From the top sphere control window, right?"

"Yes. Start at the location named Chicago-Port and find me a hospital emergency room."

She left.

I can't move him directly—can't have a tornado form in a hospital.

He opened a baseball-sized sphere between Tokyo and the vacant area where the breathing windows opened.

There was a shriek like a monster tea kettle.

He yelled, "I'm lowering the air-pressure in here. Watch your ears."

The search spiraled out a half-dozen times before he saw the man.

James opened a temporary man-sized portal and ran to it.

Eight time zones and a hard wet rain tossed him on the ground. The wind rolled him several times before he caught his balance and blinked against the stinging raid.

Where was he?

177

"American!" he shouted.

"Here!" To his left.

He crawled. No way could he stand against that wind!

"Are you injured?" Every word had to be yelled.

"Broken leg."

James could see that the man had wrapped his arm to stop it bleeding.

"Can you move?"

"Yes, but I can't walk."

"You won't need to."

James scooted next to the man, wrapped his arms around the man's chest and pressed a button on his watch.

The sphere blossomed around them, fast, but now that he'd seen the code his father wrote, he marveled at what it did. It expanded to six feet, enclosing the both of them, and then fluctuated in diameter, using the differences in altitude between the origin and the destination to detect changes in the enclosed mass, adding a safety margin so nothing important, like a foot, would be left behind. At the same time the computer bank at Base adjusted the destination location so that no significant masses, other than air, would overlap.

The result had two men, a lot of wet air, and a half-sphere of rock, dirt and concrete materializing in the base. The concrete surface under them was now tilted at a steep angle and they rolled off onto the gravel floor. The sphere collapsed, returning the concrete and most of the rock and dirt back to its origin.

"Ehhh!" cried the policeman in pain. His broken leg had twisted.

"Sorry. We'll get you home easier. Just lie there."

James got to his feet.

"Do you have that hospital yet?" he yelled.

"Just another minute."

The policeman gasped, "Who are you?"

His mother was walking up. She kneeled down to check his makeshift bandage. "I am Empress Diana. I'll need your name and address, so we can check up on you later."

"Fred Hobert. 456 Yesel Lane, Springdale."

James moved over to the closest computer screen to enter in the information, and to quickly tag the man's wristwatch. His fingers were wet and slipped on the keyboard.

"You should be okay. I apologize for this." Diana's voice changed slightly, "Tell your people that we are doing everything we can to get things under control. Tell those who poisoned my husband to put their affairs in order."

He heard the steel in her voice, and nodded.

"Ready," called Oriel.

Diana stood up. "Wait just a moment." She picked up a fat envelope from a table and handed it to the man. "A little cash to cover your immediate needs. We'll get back to you after the emergency." She nodded to Oriel, and the policeman and a pile of gravel appeared in a Chicago emergency room.

James asked, "What was that you gave him?"

His mother shrugged, "Ten thousand dollars. I found a file cabinet over there labeled, 'Laundered Money'. It really is too. Everything looks slightly faded."

"Dollars?"

"All kinds, I guess. And a stack of those yellow imperials."

James stomach growled, "Oriel, I am starved. Could you hop over to Paris and get us some food?"

She smiled, "*Certainement.*"

They found a stack of euros and James coached her through reprogramming her watch for her home and Base.

"And don't try carrying the food back with you—not until you have your world-legs. Come back, and then pull it here after you."

She nodded, grinned, and faded off to Paris.

James walked over to the printer.

His mother asked, "How much do you trust her, son?"

"Enough. Mom, if anyone could have succeeded at this by doing everything himself, it was Dad."

She nodded, "He didn't trust me."

"That's different. He was protecting us."

"He didn't trust me to risk my life for his dream."

James didn't know what to say. Oriel wanted to be a part of this—he would stake his life that she wouldn't betray them. If he was wrong, he hoped he'd never find out.

The paper in his hand gave him a way past the uncomfortable silence. He held it up.

"An Interpol agent made this list of all of Dad's agents—at least all of them that were arrested. I suspect that not a one of them knows anything important about teleportation, but they shouldn't be left in the hands of the government interrogators. Do you think we could rescue them?"

She took it. "I still feel those handcuffs."

106

"Gravel?" asked one of the black-suited agents. There were a dozen of them in the briefing room.

The Admiral looked at him sharply, "Is that important?"

"I seem to recall something about gravel when I was reviewing the hospital records looking for our subject."

"Follow it up."

The man left.

"Continue."

"Officer Hobert's statement listed the older woman as Diana, Empress of Earth. No names for the other two.

"He also reports that Empress Diana believes her husband was poisoned and is intent on tracking down those who did it."

"Anything else."

"Not at this time. He is sedated after minor surgery on his leg."

"Dismissed."

The room cleared.

So, there are still more of them. Hobert was already a news story—no chance of silencing him. They would get the poisoning rumor soon enough. *We will need to skew that a bit. Teargas? Something like that.*

He looked again at the wall map they had made of the Mt. Rushmore underground base. How long would it take to drill a shaft down to that depth?

Too long. I've just got to hope they make another mistake.

107

Ngarta clung to the ladder he had constructed out of a palm tree, with stakes driven into the sides. It balanced precariously on the pile of rocks he'd carried one by one up from the shoreline. The opening in the rock, with its **EXIT** sign was almost within reach.

He pushed himself up another step, and it was in sight.

There was a man-sized, perfectly spherical cavity inside the huge stone ball. Inside, he could see something that looked like controls. Hurriedly, he climbed another step, and jumped into the opening, even as his ladder skidded against the rock and fell hard to the ground.

I am here. I made it.

But where had he arrived? It was a simple stone cave, with an inch of water at the bottom. The controls, when he saw them, gave him a sinking feeling in the bottom of his stomach.

There was a spin wheel, like from a simple child's game. He tapped the arrow, and it spun freely. Seven zones marked with a pencil; Africa, Antarctica, Asia, Australia, Europe, North America, and South America.

The only other thing was a red button, plainly glued to the side of the rock.

It was plain what it was, a cruel joke—on him. This was not an exit, just a child's pretend version of a teleporter machine.

He looked carefully out the opening. His ladder was far below, and to jump down to the rock pile was to invite death.

He looked again to the destination wheel. *Anywhere in the world.* He didn't feel like laughing.

The water at his feet, a little muddied by his well-worn shoes—how long could that keep him alive? He was already starved.

In frustration, he spun the wheel again, and stabbed at the button.

108

James paced the aisles of computers, unable to sit down while he ate. The ham sandwich on a hard baguette tasted wonderful. He had been lavish with his praise for Oriel when she returned with sandwiches and a large plate of pastries.

She apologized for taking so long. "I called my mother and told her I would be on vacation, and then called my store to tell them I had to take off to help my sick mother."

The two women sat down to eat, discussing how to arrange the rescue of the imperial agents.

James couldn't sit still. Dad was still out there somewhere, dead or alive. His brain was churning. He had surveyed a good portion of the computer system his father had built. Long years of looking over his father's programming had really paid off.

And then, when he couldn't make any more headway, he had tracked the FBI watches he had tagged, located their supervisors, and then the destination of their reports, all the way up to the FBI Emperor Task Force.

Interpol Agent Ghest had been a great find. His reports, with a knowledge of the FBI and yet with an outsider's perspective gave a great overview to the more stilted FBI reports.

And it was clear the FBI reports were deliberately leaving things out. For example, the official rosters of the task force briefing meetings never mentioned the person Ghest quoted as 'NoBadge'—some high level person who was never officially there.

It was NoBadge who first leaked the idea that the Emperor had gone silent. It was NoBadge who knew exactly what was going on about the arrests of the imperial agents.

James tagged everyone he could find, but NoBadge had not attended the task force meeting when he had eavesdropped.

From Ghest's reading of the man, NoBadge would poison his own mother if he needed to.

James stopped in his tracks. On one of the computer racks, there was a sticky note, in his father's handwriting, "Power supply let out the magic smoke. Don't turn it back on unless you open the air portal."

The tall rack-mount computer stood black, unlike the others that had a nice set of indicator lights blinking on their front chassis.

One of the mirrored computers failed. Dad just left it sitting.

James could understand that. His father had to have worked day and night to do all the things he had done here at Base. When this one failed, the others took up the slack, and there was no time to fix computers.

When did this happen?

He dropped the rest of his sandwich and unplugged the dead computer's network cable, isolating it from the rest of the systems. These things were arranged in five-computer banks. He stepped over to the next bank and powered down one at random. Power supplies were plug-in units, designed for quick field replacement. He unplugged it and had the original failed computer booting up within three minutes.

His father had several carts with fat rubber tires that could handle the gravel. He chose one of the half-dozen computer terminals that weren't in use and wheeled it over to the isolated computer.

When it came up, the system was slightly confused by its missing brothers, and it took additional time to correct hard disk errors caused by its abrupt power loss.

But soon enough, it was up.

It thinks it is three weeks ago. Module 'crashandburn' was still in the library.

Flying fingers dug into the code. As he thought, the encryption password was there in clear text, 'The man who insists that everyone understand him will always be disappointed.'

I could have guessed that one, given enough time.

The code also included the transport code originating at his watch and dropping him at location 'St. Matthew', a hospital, obviously.

He opened another window and scrolled through the locations. St. Matthew was there. It hadn't been on the main system, he would have noticed it.

He tried to open a monitor window to St. Matthew, but there was an error. Isolated from the network, this computer wasn't connected to the teleporter hardware either.

James grabbed the sticky note from the computer and wrote down the co-ordinates of St. Matthew's Hospital.

"Mom! I've got a hospital!"

Back at his usual screen, he programmed in the new location and added it to his watch's menu.

"What are you going to do?" asked his mother.

"I'm going to go get him."

"No. You almost got blown away by that hurricane. Look before you leap. I don't want to lose you too."

His fingers vibrated against the keys. "Okay." She was right.

He opened a monitor window to the hospital emergency room. Women in white uniforms were working at computer terminals. He moved into a potted plant where he could see the screens as a lady worked, admitting someone for a broken arm.

It was painfully slow, but he was able to watch as she switched menus and had to type in her login and password.

That was all he needed. He flew his viewpoint around the neighboring offices, until he found an unattended terminal.

"Mom, help me with this." He opened a medium sized sphere. He reached through, pulling the terminal, mouse and keyboard and all through to Base. He left only the network cable, carefully shrinking the hole down to its size and making sure it was positioned out of sight.

They plugged the monitor into Base power and brought it up. "Let me have that," said his mother. James hesitated but got out of the chair.

"It's been twenty years since I worked at a hospital—a volunteer worker—but it looks like the software has hardly changed a bit."

She logged in, and quickly navigated to the admissions records. "There."

An unconscious man had been discovered at the entrance to the hospital, resting on a small pile of gravel. He was admitted as a John Doe and placed on a ventilator when his coma deepened.

She said, "No."

"What is it?"

"He is being checked out, now!" She pointed to the spot on the cluttered screen.

James found the room number. He opened a viewpoint and flew up to the fifth floor.

"I don't like this," said a man in scrubs.

"I'm sorry, but this is national security." The man in the black suit was holding a badge. "My associates are handling the paperwork as we speak. Arrange a gurney. We will be leaving immediately."

The doctor hesitated, but then hurried out.

"Davis, put your pistol to his head." The other black suit complied. "If anything, and I mean anything, starts to happen, pull that trigger."

He nodded, and arranged the covers to hide the gun.

James and his mother watched helplessly as more agents arrived and wheeled him out to a waiting ambulance.

"I can't get a sphere around him fast enough. And as likely as not, the guy with the gun would come too."

"I know." She put her hand on his shoulder.

Rescue

109

Oriel asked, "Can't you go inside the gun and remove the bullets?"

James shook his head. "I can't. Those guys ... I've been reading reports. I...."

His mother said, "We aren't going to do anything yet. I've been up thirty some hours, and so have you. They are keeping him alive, for whatever reason, so we need to let them do that. That rig they have over his face, it is keeping him breathing. If we pulled him out, we could kill him.

"James, get some sleep. When it's time to move, I want you fresh. I'll stay here. I know how to drive this thing now and I will keep out of sight."

He nodded. Oriel went with him, as the Empress stayed at the screen.

There was one bed, and he sat down on it—his father's bed.

"I will come back and check on you in a little while."

"No, wait," he said, holding out his hand for her. Oriel sat beside him. "Thank you for coming to help. This is too big a job. My father tried to do it all himself, and it may have killed him. I feel dead myself."

"I understand. My father is dead, and I can remember that time. It is very much like now. You must sleep, I know this. I will bring some more food in a little while, and we will rescue your father, and rescue all those agents."

She kissed him, and slipped out of his hand.

He was asleep before she had gone five steps.

110

Oriel scanned the status board. There was always something new to deal with. She glanced through the items, turning off the alarms before they had a chance to sound.

One caught her eye. "Island Exit activated, South America," followed by a set of coordinates. Later she would look at it.

Diana was sitting beside the other screen, her hand resting on the mouse, doing nothing. It was the picture of Oriel's own mother, as she had waited beside the bed of her father before the cancer took him.

Rebellion flared a little. *I hope they don't just wait there until he dies!*

Maybe they are too close to him. Too afraid to move.

After disposing of the most critical items on the status board, she walked over to Diana.

The lady looked tired, and worn out. Not at all like the Empress of the Earth. She smiled at Oriel.

"No change. They have him in a private room—with a nurse and three gunmen."

Oriel pulled up another chair. "Is there any chance they have seen the monitor?"

"I don't know. No one has reacted. I keep the peephole tiny and hide in the shadows. They can't hear us talk, can they?"

Oriel shook her head. "No. The sphere goes to a camera off in some rock chamber, James told me. It is just like a television when we see it on the screen.

"Do you want me to watch awhile, while you get some sleep?"

Diana put her hand across her face, massaging the aches. "No. Not for awhile. I can't lose him again."

They sat in silence.

One of the gentle alarms went off several minutes later.

Oriel got up and said, "I'll take care of that, and then go get some food. Is there anything you want?"

Diana shook her head. "Thanks for sitting with me. I kept wishing for my mother. But I couldn't bring her into this. We all might be killed.

"I guess I sound like Bob."

111

The Admiral listened to the report, frustrated at the man. Years ago, he had given up paper reports. Everything had to be done face to face. No paper trails, no way for subordinates to hide behind cut and paste wordage.

"Is there anything there?" he demanded.

The technician shook his head. "I can't tell. The room is supposed to be radio secure, but I get some slight noise. I did a manual sweep of the room and I thought I had something, but it turned out to be a wristwatch. I was ready to confiscate it, but when I checked my watch, I detected the same noise. They are tiny computers, after all."

Forsythe dismissed the man. It was frustrating, knowing that there was someone still running the teleporters—more reports were coming in all the time of systems being reactivated—and not knowing if they were aware he had their Emperor.

Being a hidden power had its advantages, but it also had its drawbacks. *How can I threaten them with his death, if they don't know I have him? I can't go to the media. And if I am still as hidden as I pay my people to be, they won't even know I'm here.*

But, there was always the second plan. And if that worked, then things would be different indeed.

112

Mayor Norris of Big Lake pointed to the ripple in the fast flowing stream moving over the spillway.

"I think it's cutting under the concrete apron. If that weakens, I worry."

The town had nothing like an engineering department, but Jess Folsom had been around when the dam had been built. He nodded. "I don't think it was ever designed to handle this much flow. A big thunderstorm, maybe, but that was all. Can't we stop it?"

The Mayor shrugged. "I have no way to contact him, if he doesn't pick up his money. We could go public, but I don't know what the feds would do to us. Local people know this is Emperor work, but none of the big news people have paid us any attention."

Jess looked over at the spillway again. "Which is worse?"

The creek was bank full already, winding its way down the valley. No one had ever considered the idea of flood-plain building restrictions. For the first time in history, the highway into town had water flowing over the asphalt. If the dam broke, nothing would be left.

"You're right, Jess. Get some people and make some sandbags, and then I'll call KLAS-TV in Las Vegas."

"Sandbags? Make 'em out of what?"

"Plastic trash bags, I guess. Use your imagination."

113

Oriel snapped awake. She had stepped back to her apartment and on impulse, had called her mother, just to hear her voice. They had talked a few minutes—she was always worried about her little girl off in wicked Paris. Oriel had let fall a hint that she was seeing someone.

That had started a marathon questioning session. "Yes, he is nice. No, we haven't had sex yet. Yes, he is respectable. He has even introduced me to his mother. No, no more questions. I love you Mother."

She had collapsed on the bed, for just a minute, and from clock on the wall, she had slept for three hours. What must they be thinking back at Base?

She changed clothes and headed to pick up the food.

114

James had several screens open before him. His father was still breathing. Oriel had jumped out of her bed, rattling off high speed French as she realized she had overslept. He closed that one. She would be back soon, he was sure.

In another window, he was reading the decrypted logs. When he took over from his mother, and sent her off to sleep, he carefully located the exact byte where the encrypted and clear text parts of the log met and sliced out the encrypted part, used the password and then rejoined them.

The log file was fascinating reading.

It started with plain text. His father kept a log of his experiments before he discovered the teleportation. He had been bitter about his layoff. James hadn't realized how much so. His father had always been a quiet man, keeping his angers to himself. It had been quite a shock to learn what the man was capable of.

So that was what the skyrocket was all about! I wish I'd been home when it finally worked.

The details of the lightning trap had been removed from the log, edited out manually. There were other gaps too. Several times, his father rambled on about the theory of how the spheres worked, and then just when it started to get interesting, the entry would just stop, sometimes in the middle of a sentence.

But the discovery of the teleportation was there in minute detail—his trials and errors, what worked and what didn't. There was a wealth of practical details.

And then, he read the incident of Willis. The death of their dog changed the tone of his log entries. From that moment on, he was serious. For days, the entries were more an argument with himself about the idea of burning his notebooks and smashing the apparatus.

James sat up in his chair.

> "This evening, while working on the tracking
> system, I saw something, that as a father, I wish I
> had not seen."

There was more. Enough to bring the memory of that moment with Suzie back in sharp detail.

Oriel called out, "I'm back."

James collapsed the window, his heart beating loudly.

"Hi." He swiveled in the chair, to see her walking up behind him. "Have a nice nap?"

She blushed, "Sorry."

"No problem. I just checked on you when you were late. Better to be safe than sorry." He noticed the bag in her arms. "What did you bring me?"

They ate next to the screen, talking in low tones so as not to disturb Diana.

"I've been reading my father's logs—looking for hints as to how to pull him out of there."

"Any luck?"

"Not yet. I'm not that far into the history. Did you know that the first version of teleportation was deadly? You went through it and your blood came out the other way."

She shivered. "I'm glad I didn't know that."

"I'll keep reading. Do you have any ideas?"

"For your father, no, other than to distract the guards long enough to pull him out. For the agents that have been arrested, I think that should be easier, if we had a place to send them."

"Don't bring them here?"

Oriel shook her head sadly. "Your father was wise in this. There are many agents, I am certain some of them are working for their governments."

"What makes you think so?"

"Human nature. It is weak. Look at this." She reached into her bag and pulled out a stack of euro notes of various sizes.

"I could not earn this much money in a year. And yet it is like dirty napkins in this place. These dropboxes are full of cash, and we are too busy to bother to launder them. There are a dozen payments we haven't bothered to pick up.

"People will make compromises with their souls for this.

"You shouldn't have brought me here. I lust after this." She dropped the money back into her bag.

He smiled at her. "But sometimes you have to just trust people."

She nodded, "Yes, but not all these agents. The odds are against it."

"We still have to rescue them. They are my father's agents. We owe them."

"What about this Archer? He is hidden and safe."

115

From his terrace, Archer could watch the boats on their regular trek across North Sound where tourists could wade out on the white sandbars and feed the stingrays. He had done it a couple of times himself—although he had more of an adrenaline rush from taking off his wristwatch than he had of any fear of the evil looking creatures.

How many days will it take before I'm not afraid anymore?

There was a knock on his glass door, from the inside.

A young man stood inside, waving at him.

Archer froze for a moment. He could run, he could greet the intruder, or he could press the button on his watch that would shift him to another one of his five hideaways.

"Are you coming in? I'd rather not come out there, if you don't mind," his visitor asked.

The voice decided him. Archer came inside and looked at the boy carefully.

"Do I know you?"

"No. But I know you. Your hair looks different."

"How did you get in here? I have an expensive security system."

The young man gave him a sardonic look. "Hardly a question Gregory Archer should ask, is it?"

"My name is Bluthman. Gerold Bluthman."

"I'm James. You work for my father."

Archer nodded, "Have a seat." He did the same.

"I had my hand on my watch, until I heard your voice. You sound very much like him. Is he alive?"

James frowned. "For the moment. We're working on his rescue. He has been poisoned and is in a coma."

Archer drew in a deep breath. "I was afraid of something like that." He reached up and removed a dark hairpiece.

"What can I do to help?"

116

"Doctor, do you have good news for me?" The Admiral expected good news from all his people. He was frequently disappointed.

"He is stabilized. I can't get him much better with my hands tied like they are."

"I don't want his recovery. Not yet. You can't hold an angry snake in your hands. You either have to let it go, or chop off its head. I much prefer him unconscious.

"You can, of course, help me tame him."

"Give me a couple of days. It's risky."

"I thought you said that he won't improve without a change of treatment. Why wait?"

The doctor paused, "Okay, *I* am not ready."

"You can be replaced."

"And it would take time to replace me! I have the drugs, but it will be a very risky dance with the dosages. Give me two days."

"One day, no more. I have my own risks to weigh."

117

"I may have just killed my son. I had no choice. He was unconscious, and the pickup was sinking in the flood. I could have dived through the portal myself, but with the blood loss, I would be unconscious and no help to anybody.

"It was the only way. I just hope he lives through the night."

James flicked on past the story of his hospitalization. Some other time, he could think about that.

I owe my life to this invention. It's as simple as that. Once I lost control of the pickup in the water, I was done for.

"James, are you okay?" Oriel asked.

"Yes. Fine. What do you need?" He closed the log window.

"Archer just sent a message. He's ready on his end."

"You have them located."

"Yes. We could do it now."

They walked over to Diana.

"Mom, I..."

"Wait just a second." She was reading something in a monitor window.

James looked over at the view of his father. He was breathing without the respirator, but he looked very thin and tired. *How many more days in this cave before I look like that?*

Diana looked up. "James, we need to move your father now."

"What's up?"

She waved at the screen. "I started following the doctor that's treating him. He gets all his orders in person, but he's a doctor and doctors keep records.

"He knows the poison, and knows what to do to bring Bob out of it, but he has orders not to.

"Instead, they are going to make a zombie out of him."

"What?"

"It's some kind of top secret drug treatment. It dulls certain brain centers. The doctor's boss wants to be able to be in control of my husband's mind as they wake him up. He wants to use him to gain control of the teleporters.

"But once they start the drug treatment, it permanently affects his mind! James, we have to stop him."

He nodded and looked at Oriel. "Your plan. Can you do it?"

She nodded, suddenly afraid. "The bullets?"

"It'll take me ten minutes, maybe fifteen."

"Okay, I need to change." She pressed her watch and vanished.

James felt a shiver. "Mom, get ready. Collect all the medical gear you will need. We have at least two hospitals in the database. Steal everything. We'll pay them back later."

"Okay."

"And Mom?"

"Yes."

"Be ready to handle bullet wounds as well."

Mother and son looked at each other for one long moment, and then he broke away at a run. Time was slipping away.

118

Archer sat by his pool at his Bahamian residence in Nassau. He glanced at the tables spread out with food, and the odd one with the jewelry James had him purchase.

Not that the boy had explained anything. It must run in the family.

Wait in ignorance. Well, I can do that. Doing that for the Emperor had paid very well.

119

Davis had head duty. Gun resting by the pillow, he glanced at his watch.

The doctor is due any minute now. Hancock and Lewis sat quiet and motionless. They were supposed to be on the lookout for anything unusual, and to put backup slugs into the body if he were taken out.

Fat chance of that. Davis was smug. He knew the secrets of the cats. There was a place to go, where your mind and body were still, and yet on the edge of an explosion.

Thump-dub. Thump-dub.

That's my heart beating. I'm like an Indian mystic, feeling every part of my body.

Hancock adjusted his glasses. Lewis blinked.

Knock. Knock.

The door began to open.

A bright light beamed into the room, silhouetting a beautiful young girl in a pale, translucent dress. She smiled at him. His heartbeat sped up.

Davis blinked. *This isn't right.* He lurched to his feet, unable to take his eyes off of her. Hancock and Lewis were stumbling.

She held out her hand to him.

No! This isn't right. The prisoner?

He turned and saw that the subject's feet, his legs and torso had already gone.

Like a tiger, he aimed at the head, and pulled the trigger.

Click. His gun didn't fire! Cotton filled his head. Hearing was a distant buzz. He fainted.

Oriel smiled to see all three of them fall to the ground. Two of them tried to fire their guns, but James had been on the job. The bullets were duds.

The Emperor's head vanished, and the meter wide sphere they had used to remove him collapsed.

"Hold it right there!"

Behind her. Blinking against the sudden daylight where there should never be daylight, another of the black-suited agents had his gun trained on her.

She forced a smile, one she had practiced in the mirror for years. "Don't do that," she said in a gentle voice.

Skidding into the corridor, another agent appeared, and *Bang!* snapped off a shot.

She saw the bullet, just for an instant, as it stopped in mid-flight and ricocheted off an invisible bubble between her and them.

The cautious agent groaned and fell.

"I told you," she said, the instant before she vanished.

120

Oriel stumbled at the time zone change, but James was there to grab her.

Her smile was for him only, and he pulled her into a passionate kiss.

She gasped, at last. "Merci."

He straightened, "Sorry. It must have been the dress."

The smile brightened, "Of course. Why do you think I bought it?"

"Are you okay?"

"*Je suis parfait.* They fell on their faces. How much blood did you drain from them?"

"Just over a liter apiece. I remember what it was like."

His heartbeat was racing. Seeing her like that when he had been anemic would have put him on the ground too.

He released her. "I've got to check on my father."

James headed quickly toward the bedroom.

He skidded to a halt in the doorway. His mother stood besides a balding doctor, stethoscope in play.

She looked up and smiled, "You said to steal what I needed. I decided to buy him instead."

James took a step forward. The doctor nodded at him, but didn't stop from his examination.

She whispered, "This is Dr. Ray Feldstein. I worked for him some years ago. He's been pushing for a neurological clinic ever since I've known him. I decided to buy him one."

James whispered back. "Is he safe here?"

She nodded.

The doctor muttered, "Nasty, nasty stuff. Let me look at that sheet again." Diana handed over the printout she had made of the other doctor's notes.

James motioned his mother out of the room.

"Oriel and I have to get the agents out, immediately. Can you handle this end?"

She smiled, tolerantly.

He blushed, "Okay, okay. But call if you need any help."

Oriel read his smile. "The Emperor? He is okay."

"Mom brought in a doctor. She is confident."

"Now the agents?"

"Now the agents."

They headed for their consoles. James lagged a little, looking her over. He just couldn't get over her dress.

121

Archer noticed the lady in prison orange materialize next to the pool.

"Ah, Mrs. Leffer. So good to see you." He took her hand. As a young black man in darker prison clothes appeared, still sitting in a chair, he pointed her toward the guesthouse. "You will find more suitable clothes that way."

Archer spread his hands.

"Mr. Jones. Happy to have you here."

"What's going on?" He jumped out of his chair, looking around the hedged yard.

"You have been rescued. You will find a wide selection of better clothes in the house." He pointed the way.

By that time three more people had arrived. Only one had civilian clothes. They all embraced the promise of untainted clothes with decided eagerness.

James appeared last of all.

Archer asked, "How did it go?"

"Very smooth. We took the precaution of delaying the report of my father's disappearance."

"Oh?"

James grinned, but it wasn't a pleasant grin. "Quite a number of FBI agents, police, dirty doctors and assorted spooks simultaneously went visiting a certain tropical island."

122

Rudy Ghest walked ashore, shaking the salt water out of his gun. That seemed to be the same course of action of thirty or more other men.

We seem to be the best-armed group to wade out of the water since D-day.

Many of them were familiar. Practically all of the FBI's Emperor Task Force were represented.

He also recognized NoBadge. Quite a contingent was collecting around him.

"Look at this!" called out one of the FBI agents. He held up the yellow wrappings of a UN food package. "At least he isn't planning to starve us."

Rudy was the only Interpol agent. Eschewing both the FBI and black-suit parties, he walked over to meet the other few oddballs.

With so many law enforcement agents collected in one spot, there ought to be no problem. Still, he had visions of the child savages of 'Lord of the Flies'—well armed savages.

123

"Greeting to you all again. I am your host Gregory Archer, the First Agent of the Emperor."

There was a murmur of recognition. In their fine new clothes, complete with accessories such as men's and women's Rolex watches, the party looked quite high-society.

"Except for a very lucky break, I would have joined your exclusive club as a guest of the Memphis Tennessee Police. I was lucky, and now, so are you.

"May I introduce, James, the son of our Emperor."

There were a few gasps, and then a spattering of applause.

James stood very straight. Archer had provided him a tuxedo. He had a part to play. *But I'm getting rid of this suit the instant I get back to Base.*

"I am here today to apologize to you, and to thank you for the great services you have provided my father. The Empress Diana, my mother, is at this minute by the side of Emperor Robert. He was poisoned and was only rescued from near death just moments before your own release."

James could hear the response of some. Many only needed a good reason why they hadn't been rescued earlier. Others were likely still bitter.

"Your well-being has been a deep concern to us since we heard the news of your arrests.

"The empire has been lax concerning your safety. It had been the hope of my father that nations would more quickly recognize the legitimacy of the empire, and diplomatic immunity could be provided for its agents.

"We will do better. You will be compensated. We will punish those agencies who so unjustly acted against you. And we will provide protection for you and your families from future attacks."

There were cheers at that.

"Item one. The Empress Diana has ordered that all imprisoned agents be paid hazard honors of one million dollars US for each hour you were detained.

"Item two." He had to raise his voice over their cheers.

"Item two. You will be provided safe accommodations, of your own choice, anywhere in the world. First Agent Archer will be working closely with you on that. If your homes are no longer safe, families will be moved, and your wishes accommodated.

"Item three. On this table to your right, you will see an assortment of jewelry. You will each select one, and this will provide your greatest protection.

"Each piece has embedded within it a device that can transport you, in an instant, to the empire's central base. All you will have to do is call out a single word, which I will give each of you in private.

"No longer." He paused for their silence. "No longer will you be alone. If they come for you, they can't keep you. If they come for your families, agents at the base can work immediately to protect them.

"My father is correct in pursuing a diplomatic solution to your permanent safety, and when he is fully recovered he will be making strong moves to insure that. But for now, you have my personal bond as Crown Prince that we won't let you down again."

124

"While I was watching one of the James Bond movies, 'Diamonds are Forever', I had the notion that what the world really needed to protect itself from the catastrophe of unchecked teleportation, was some kind of special police force, ready to snap into action, with the technology and tactics needed to keep the common citizen from harm.

"But how to do that? I don't even know how to detect the spheres remotely, and obviously that would be a necessary tool. The instant I reveal the technology to the world, the cat is out of the bag, and the damage is done.

"Then it occurred to me that I could reverse the roles. I could play the bad guy, the Blofeld, and scare the world community into developing the tools and tactics to defeat me. The world would get used to the idea of teleportation gradually, and if I were nimble enough, I could string it out for years.

"Of course, at best I would live my life out in prison, but people are treated worse for much less. It is my invention, my responsibility. The other researchers have the same theories that I started with. How long until someone else invents it independently?

"I could destroy it now, burn my notes, but what would that accomplish?

"The first person to use teleportation will be the seed crystal around which a new civilization crystallizes. Can I do a better job at phasing in this new thing than every one else? Certainly I can do a better job than some. I can think of a dozen ways to kill everyone on earth. So can the next guy. If I can protect the earth, and I turn down the chance, then what am I?"

James closed the log window.

He got up and went to the bedroom. A sphere blocked the doorway. The first thing James had done was to give Dr. Feldstein a semi-permanent portal back to his office, and he was in and out all the time. The bedroom had become an invisible annex to the county hospital where he worked.

James changed the settings and walked through it, then reset them. No matter how trustworthy the doctor was, security measures had to be followed.

His father raised his hand. James grasped it.

"You look terrible, Emperor."

He whispered something. He was weak and the treatment was still in the early stages.

"I have been reading the logs. I think I understand what you were trying to do. We are all behind you. You won't be alone anymore."

125

Crunch. James scowled at the gravel underfoot.

I could grow to hate this place. It's like living in a cellar. Like a bombshelter.

Oh, well—it is a bombshelter.

He walked the length of the rock gallery. It was dark at the edges, far from the tall lamps that his father had brought in for work near the computers.

The little bulldozer startled him, sleeping in the dark like a menacing dragon.

I can't let Dad live out his life here either. It would be like a life sentence in prison.

The cart and the dead power supply cluttering the aisle between the rows of computers were annoying. More stuff to do.

He headed back.

Oriel was a vision of perfection, hunched over a computer screen.

James came up beside her and placed his hand on her shoulder.

She smiled. "Can you take this for awhile? I need to change. These are hardly work clothes."

He lifted his hand from her skin, reluctantly. "Sure. It may be some time before we get a strike on our fishing expedition."

She got up and kissed him on the cheek before vanishing.

The status board was still very cluttered. A whole set of the alarms had just been deferred. *Hardly businesslike, but maybe when we get back on an even keel, we can make some changes.*

He clicked the CNN button and moved the noisy colorful window to one side of the screen while he worked on the queue.

There was a news summary, talking about the disappearances of the agents and of the police and FBI agents. The missing law enforcement people had triggered a terrorist state of emergency in the US and Britain. There was the feeling that the Emperor had struck back for the arrest of his agents, and there was fear that they were dead.

True to form, reporters had invaded the houses of wives and parents to poke them for visible emotional response that could be entertainment for the viewers.

The news shifted to a summary of the disasters of the last week that were directly caused by the teleportation. Chicago and Tokyo were still picking up the pieces of the storm. Then they started covering the flood in Big Lake Nevada.

"What is this?" James cried, and rapidly started searching the status list.

126

The Mayor of Big Lake was knee deep in water, with a safety rope around his waist. He and another man on the other side of the spillway were trying to float a log crosswise into the most turbulent part of the flow. The sandbags hadn't worked well, and the water was still rising.

Bill Norris knew disaster was coming, and that it was his fault.

The creek was causing considerable damage down where it met the highway. Road traffic was entirely cut off, and the channel was widening by the hour. Three buildings were having their foundations undercut and they would be lucky if that was all.

The spillway was eroding. Its channel was deepening, drawing a greater flow of water, and giving it more turbulence to cut the channel even deeper. It was a feedback system that would likely go catastrophic at any time.

He knew it was a lost cause, but if they could find a way to slow the flow through the channel, something could be done to save the dam.

Thunder? No. It was a voice, magnified as if by a huge loud speaker system.

"This is Imperial Disaster Control. Please get everyone out of the spillway."

Jess and his crew looked at the mayor. He waved them back. *Yes, get clear.*

Up on the firm side of the dam, the news crews, who had gathered to get a good shot of the collapse, hurried to get their cameras rolling.

He could see it starting. The flow of water was pushed aside, as if by a giant inflatable, invisible, balloon. In less than a minute, the water was halted, standing up by itself, just like in the Ten Commandments movie.

The roar of the spillway, which had grown so loud and so constant that they had stopped talking to each other, was stilled.

Jess yelled from across the spillway. "I can see it."

Norris could too.

The sphere was perfectly clear, yet visible, just as if it were made of a thin shell of ultrapure crystal. The edge was just a few feet away. He stepped closer, and touched it. Hard as a rock, and cold. He hit it. No vibration, no ring. It was like hitting a mountain.

The ground that was enclosed by the sphere was starting to form frost. Vapor was streaming away from the exposed spillway and vanishing.

"Mayor Norris." It was like the voice of a giant that had plugged the leak with his thumb. "The Emperor apologizes to you and the community for this lapse. The water transfer has been halted and the lake level will be lowered to a safe level. We will be in touch concerning damage downstream."

He looked carefully at the water level. *Is it dropping? Maybe. I just hope he doesn't go too low. We still need the water.*

127

Oriel had returned, in sweater and slacks.

"How did you do that?" she asked.

James leaned back in the chair, his face solemn. "The same way we deflected that bullet. Make a sphere with one end on the ground and the other a thousand miles up in space—but with the elevation compensation turned off. The bullet, and the water in this case, would have to climb the equivalent of 500 miles to enter the sphere, so it bounces instead. This one took a lot of energy because of the mass of the soil I had to include inside the sphere."

He stared at the new warning on the status board.

"Energy Reserves Low." Maybe the condition would be resolved when he was able to release the sphere blocking the spillway.

Oriel looked at the screen. "James, this is my fault. This Big Lake was one of the alerts I saw. I just turned off the noise. I had no idea it was so critical."

He nodded, "We need to review every single thing in the queue, and process them. No one knows which are critical and which are not. Only my father, and maybe Archer know what most of these even are."

He looked up at her face. "Don't take it too hard. It's impossible to stop an avalanche, and that's what we're trying to do. There are only three of us, and trained operators should man this status board 24 hours a day. I have no idea how my father kept it up.

"Something has to change."

Traitor

128

Kurt Sommer held the gold moneyclip in his hands, looking at it from all sides. It certainly looked natural. The circuitry had to be in the thick part, and that crevice had to be the microphone to pick up the trigger word. His was "bullfrog". Not a word he was likely to use in ordinary conversation.

First Agent Archer had been very accommodating when he had chosen to get an apartment under a fake name in New York. With his new wealth, the Plaza came to mind, and as soon as he said it, Archer had the arrangements made.

He had listened attentively to the suggestions Archer had given him about subtle changes in his appearance to avoid being recognized.

Not that it was a real concern for him.

He wrapped the moneyclip in a handkerchief and sealed it inside a wide-mouthed thermos jug, and wrapped that in layers of cloth before stuffing it into a backpack. There was no way sound could get to it now.

It was a nice, sunny day in Central Park, and he walked the trails until he came to a park bench in the shade of some trees.

A few minutes later, another man sat beside him. He began twisting his ring on his finger, like a nervous habit.

Sommer relaxed. "I love this time of year."

"Before things get too hot."

They nodded, the recognition signals over.

The stranger said, "We were worried when you vanished. But I guess we should have been more worried if you hadn't."

"It was a lovely trip. Somewhere in the Caribbean maybe, or the Bahamas. I think it was Archer's house. I've got it all written down in my backpack."

The other man was listening to something. Sommer nodded, he was probably wired.

"The Chief asks if you have a new assignment."

"Not yet, but I was told by Crown Prince James that I would be contacted within the month."

"Crown Prince, eh? Anything else, other than the report?"

"Oh yes! Imperial agents have been given a teleport gadget disguised as jewelry. Mine is a moneyclip, wrapped up in the backpack. It's sound sensitive. Say 'bullfrog' and you are transported to the secret base."

His contact was silent again for a moment.

"Great work."

129

Diana, Oriel and James listened to the rest of the conversation being picked up by Sommer's new Rolex watch.

Their faces were grim.

Diana shook her head, "So they would send an assassin in on a possible suicide mission to get us. These people are cold."

"*Traître!*" Oriel spat. "He should be killed."

James sympathized with the feeling. But saying it and doing it were different things.

"We should do nothing. We're still not recognized as a legal government. He is not an active threat. It'll be enough to notify

Archer and steer clear of him. His moneyclip is just a piece of jewelry, after all."

Diana disagreed, "We can't let him get away with it. Like it or not, we depend on these agents, and if they can get away with sticking a knife in our backs, then we will regret it later."

"A public flogging?" he asked, half joking.

She nodded, "Something like that."

James waited as she thought something out.

Oriel's eyes sparkled. *She's ready for revenge, too.*

The idea disturbed him. It was too much like uncontrolled power. Wasn't the whole idea of the Empire to bring a tight control over teleportation, so that society could mature into it? That was Dad's idea, at least.

If Mom goes past the line, I'll have to object and bring Dad into this.

Diana asked, "This meeting was recorded, right?"

James nodded. "All the agent watches are. The words go through the speech recognition system and that's what triggered this alert, but everything is recorded."

"Good."

130

James wheeled a television monitor into the bedroom.

"I thought you might want to watch this."

His father nodded. He was weak, but his mind had been clear enough when they brought the proposal to him. James had insisted. He was still the Emperor.

But with a couple of his suggestions, the idea was approved.

The background details had already been taken care of. Sommer's contacts had been tagged and were being monitored by the automated systems. The moneyclip had been removed before they had a chance to examine it to preserve that illusion.

"Why don't we send them to the island?" Oriel had asked.

"No," objected James. "We are already in a public opinion mess about the people already missing. Sommer is a traitor. He signed up with the Emperor. He is ours. The others are just spooks doing their job. Until they attack us, we shouldn't do a thing."

The time approached.

The TV announcer said, "We have just received an announcement from the Emperor that an important announcement will be made at nine AM at the Sheep Meadow in Central Park. We have a film crew on the way and we will be covering it live here on WCBS."

Oriel came to the door. She bowed her head toward the Emperor.

"Come on in." His voice was weak, but his smile was genuine.

"Diana has already started. She had to warn the crowd away," Oriel reported.

The TV coverage wasn't long in appearing. There was a crowd, and more were gathering.

James asked, "Are we sure Sommer is unaware of what's happening? He lives within sight of this."

Oriel nodded. *"C'est perfection.* He is taking a shower."

James pointed, "There. It's starting."

On the screen a giant, hundred-foot tall ball of granite appeared out of thin air and slammed down in to the meadow. The ground tremor knocked some of the closer people off their feet. There were shrieks of panic.

The TV commentator started talking, saying nothing that wasn't already visible.

James turned to his father. "Those things are impressive looking."

He nodded. "I made them for energy storage. Carved a bunch out of the Himalayas."

A familiar voice echoed over the scene. "This is the Empress Diana. This is a public notice that Kurt Sommer, formerly an agent of the Emperor, has been fired for treason."

There was a shout from the crowd as a tiny naked figure appeared on the top of granite globe.

"Kurt Sommer! For treasonous activities against the Emperor, you are hereby discharged from imperial service. All benefits and payments are forfeit."

James whispered to his father. "We have taken care of that. We've even cleaned out his dresser drawers and cancelled his room."

Then the recording started. Amplified so all could hear it, Sommer and his contact discussed how they might send an assassin in to kill everyone at the imperial base.

"That will loop for a day—give everyone a chance to hear it."

The TV cameraman zoomed in close to see the naked man, still wet from his shower and shivering, sit down on the top of the ball.

Oriel asked, "How long will he stay there?"

James shrugged, "Until they can get a crane or a helicopter in there to remove him."

She jeered, "I hope he jumps."

James asked, "Dad? Should we remove the ball once this is over?"

"No. Leave it. New Yorkers will love it."

131

The Admiral chatted quietly with the man from Russia. His people had found a comfortable rock where he could sit.

"Yes, we verified it. His cash deliveries arrive deep inside the mountain only a few hundred feet from the teleportation central. Some agency, I can't say which, left a small explosive device to be picked up and it went off.

"I bet they were shaken up a bit. It's a shame nobody had the foresight to leave them something a bit more powerful. That would have taken them out."

"Then why haven't you?"

Forsythe waved his hands. "It's under a national shrine. Statues of beloved presidents. Nobody in our country would dare make that move, no matter what the benefit."

"Then no one else would either. Not if it would anger the US."

Forsythe nodded wisely, "Yes, I would hate to be the one who rid the world of this 'emperor', especially if the bomb could be traced back to me."

He let the other man see a dangerous smile. "But they haven't stopped me. My hands are busy—always busy."

132

"Hi, Dad."

"James. How are you doing?"

"Poorly, I think."

"What's the problem?" He clicked the control button on the new the hospital bed they had moved in for him. It raised him up to a sitting position.

James stood close, a frown on his face and tapping his hand nervously on the bed's railing.

"Dad, I think you are wrong."

"How so?"

"I've read your logs. I understand what you were trying to do. The problem is that you can't be a Blofeld. It isn't in you to be a supervillian. Oh, you've got the secret base, the ultimatum to the UN—but you don't have an evil bone in your body.

"As far as I can tell, in spite of what you were telling yourself, from the very beginning you tried to set up an honorable, respectable business. You declared a billion dollar tax and then as far as I can see, you paid for everything you took."

"With funny money."

"And then went to great lengths to give value to the imperials.

"You may have called yourself an Emperor just to get a rise out of people, but that's what you became. You have dictated policies to all nations on the earth, and you have the technological high ground to give you the power to enforce those policies if you so desire."

"A dictator."

"A monarch."

Bob Hill looked very tired. He shook his head.

"Sorry son, I can't control what the people of the world do."

"Sorry, Emperor, but that is exactly what you are doing. You dictate exactly when and where teleportation happens. You're not going to turn it all over to them, and you know why. You thought it all out and wrote it down in your logs.

"Until a new world culture crystallizes around your pattern, the world will be too immature to handle widespread use of the teleporters.

"We still need the special police force who can handle rogue teleporters. We still need to keep our hands on the technology. We still need to guide businesses and governments into the safe ways to use it.

"The planet earth needs one controlling government to phase in teleportation—each country making its own rules is nonsense. Maybe there is some honorable and wise government out there we could turn it all over to. I wouldn't bet on it.

"Why not make it real? Be the Emperor, for the rest of your life. Mom has done great under pressure. She can be a great Empress. And to be honest, I have done pretty well myself."

Bob Hill was silent for several minutes. James sat quietly beside him. He had made his pitch.

"What should we do differently?" the Emperor asked finally.

133

The four of them sat in a circle. Bob relished getting out of bed finally, even if he was still confined to the wheelchair.

"James has convinced me that we are on a down-hill slide. We have to improve our public image, and that means going public."

"How public?" asked Diana.

"Television cameras in our face. *People* magazine. Hours upon hours of interviews with the media. The public likes a royal family. Let's give them one."

"Oh. I can't do that. Not dressed like this."

"Not today, Mom." James laughed. "We have a lot of preparation to do. For one thing we have to make it safe."

Diana shook her head, "Still...."

Oriel patted her hand. "I know people. In Paris." She looked at the Emperor. "We will need to go shopping."

James agreed, "Better now than after our press conference."

134

"It's two AM, James," complained his mother.

"I know, but we have a full day ahead of us. Learn to embrace jet-lag, because you will get a lot of it."

Oriel was on the other side of her. "It will be okay. Once we hit the streets of Paris, you will come alive. I know this."

"Got the money?" he asked.

Oriel patted her bag.

"Okay, here we go."

They appeared at Pont Neuf, on the Seine, next to a long rack of magazine display-cases on the Left Bank.

James had timed it well. There were few people around, and no one appeared to have noticed their arrival.

"Oof. That was a big step," complained Diana. But James and Oriel had been prepared and no one fell down.

"There is my store." Oriel pointed across the bridge.

They walked together, as tourists. Oriel led them to the clothing section. This was just the first step. They had to be wearing clothes nice enough so the top designers wouldn't bar them at the door. Mother and son had been living in the clothes they wore when the crackdown occurred.

"Oriel!" There was a feminine squeal and a trio of clerks descended on them. James stepped back, instantly losing track of the rapid-fire French. They had worried about their friend, that much was certain.

They gave just a glance at the two Americans until Oriel introduced '*mes amis*' and said they were there to buy clothes.

Everything felt fine, until James noticed that one of them was staring intently at Diana. He turned to her, "Hello? *Quelle est votre nom?*"

The girl looked at him, and her eyes widened even more. She backed away.

"Oriel?" James whispered, and then nodded towards the girl.

Oriel smiled, "*Marian? Y a-t-il un problème?*"

The two girls huddled, and Oriel's face dropped. "Diana, James, come here."

They walked over to the cash register. Marian dug out a newspaper. There on the front page were pictures of Diana and

James and Robert Hill. The headline was *"NOUVELLE FAMILLE ROYALE?"*

James chuckled. "Well, it looks like we've already hit the tabloids."

He felt the TV remote control in his pocket. It had been one of Bob Hill's projects before he had been poisoned. Slightly altered so that it always emitted a trace radio signal, it was just another version of the wristwatches. This was for use in public settings, in an attempt to keep the programmed watches secret for just a little longer.

One button was for him and another for all of them. If they had to escape, he would be ready.

"Oui. C'est l'impératrice et son fils. Pouvez-vous nous aider?" Oriel spoke earnestly, begging her friend to help.

It didn't take long after that.

Assistance was called in, and James was fitted in a nice suit. Expensive or not, he couldn't tell. Jeans were more his style. But Oriel liked it.

His mother looked elegant in a yellow suit. They even did something to her hair.

But there was a crowd gathering. The word was out.

Oriel led them out of sight and nodded. James hit the button programmed with the designer she had chosen.

They walked into an elegant salon. A man was there, waiting for them. His staff lined the wall behind him.

"Empress Diana. When we got your call, I ordered every one out. We are at your disposal."

135

James took another look at himself in the mirror. *It's just another uniform.*

He shrugged his shoulders. Not nearly as padded as his football uniform, but it seemed to always look right, no matter how he stood.

The patch on his lapel took some getting used to. They had to have a logo. A plain yellow circle on the black background of his jacket looked better than some of the other ideas they had tossed around.

His father looked imposing, with a more imperial version of the same outfit. The Empress was in an entirely different style, but with the same logo and theme.

"How do I look, James?" Oriel cocked her head, looking slightly military in her dove gray version. The black was for the royal family.

"You look good."

Emperor Robert said, "Archer has the others ready. James. It's show time."

"Okay. Meet you there."

He faced the rock wall of the gallery. "That is west, I think." He took off at a sprint and was instantly on the surface, speeding across the plains, covering hundreds of miles at a step. Guiding by the sun and the sky, he slowed his pace, covering only twenty or thirty miles per step.

There. That must be Lake Michigan. He slowed still more and turned to the south. Shortly, he saw the Ohio river flick by. He shifted his course a little eastward and when he approached a city, he slowed and hunted for a highway sign. *Athens Georgia. Too far east*, he turned. *But at least I'm in the right state.*

Atlanta. He pulled out the little map he had with him and quickly stepped up to CNN Center. There were security guards, but he flickered quickly past them through the walls, carefully keeping his pace down so that he wouldn't step out past the other end of the building.

There were the studios. He paused on the floor. Several workers noticed him.

There. That is where the live broadcast comes from. He stepped in that direction and it was as if the walls were illusions, he walked right through them.

The news commentator looked at him as he materialized in front of him, right beside the cameras. A man in a headset carrying a clipboard tried to grab him, but his hand bounced off something invisible.

"Excuse me. I apologize for interrupting your news program, but the Emperor of Earth is giving a speech. In Person. Right now.

"If you would care to cover the event..." The commentator said, "Yes, I would."

"Then please stand up and come over here. Two cameras, they don't have to be wireless."

The TV studio people juggled the lights and cameras, all of it live and on camera.

"An opening will appear and surround the four of us. We will walk just a step this way. The cables can trail behind. That's okay."

James clicked something that looked like a garage door opener, and the sphere appeared as he said.

It was bright daylight, and they moved as James directed. The sphere shrunk behind them, down to about four feet, and the cables and a pair of curious heads poked through the opening.

They were set up on the wide bald peak of some granite mountain. There was a flicker twenty feet before them, and suddenly there were a dozen people dressed in the imperial theme. In the center of the group was the Emperor in a wheelchair, attended by a doctor and his Empress.

James stepped in their direction, flickering across the distance like an image captured by a strobe light. He stood by their side.

Diana spoke, and her voice echoed loud, amplified by some invisible means.

"I am Empress Diana. Much has happened in the past few days. Events have changed, and my husband has decided that the layer of secrecy can to some extent be lifted.

"This press event has been called to inform the world what has happened.

"One week ago a plan orchestrated by Retired Admiral Forsythe, formerly of the United States National Security Agency, succeeded in a goal of poisoning my husband by lacing the paper used to print imperial script with a neurotoxin, named VNE, invented by the USA.

"The Emperor collapsed, but not before activating several security measures.

"The machinery of the empire which controls the teleportation spheres went on automatic, with no controlling hand.

"To the peoples of Tokyo and Chicago, and officer Hobert, we extend our apologies for the destruction triggered by Typhoon Koppu.

"And to the people of Big Lake Nevada, we apologize for the uncontrolled water flow that almost destroyed your city.

"These near disasters would never have happened except for this unwarranted and internationally illegal attack on the person of the Emperor.

"To these cities we ask that damage estimates be sent to us by the usual channels and we will assist you with the repairs."

She paused.

"Several nations were waiting for the chance to strike against the Empire. When they suspected that the Emperor was disabled, they undertook to arrest innocent agents in our employ, whose only 'crime' was to read the newspaper."

She gave a nod to the assembled agents. Most had chosen to come.

Diana was using a voice James had heard often when growing up. He was glad she wasn't talking to him.

"Finally, when Admiral Forsythe located the hospital where the Emperor was being treated, he kidnapped my husband and held him with a pistol to his head!

"His evil scheme called for chemical brain washing using," she referred to a piece of paper, "system FHD-22, created by the CIA in an illegal chemical warfare program in 1994.

"Fortunately, members of the Royal Family and French special agent Oriel Meirieu were able to rescue the Emperor and those imperial agents illegally arrested.

"Under the care of Dr. Feldstein, my husband is well on the way to recovery, and the machinery of teleportation is back in his capable hands."

The assembled agents clapped.

She stepped back, and the Emperor rolled his wheelchair forward.

Amplified, his voice sounded strong.

"I wish to thank my rescuers, and those cooler heads who argued against this attack on the Empire.

"These attacks were motivated by national pride, and in some cases by personal greed for power. In my declaration to the UN, I stated my claim to this imperial throne, and I have the power to enforce this claim.

"In news articles and in discussions both public and private, the potential for destruction that can be caused by teleportation has been widely discussed. How many different ways can humanity be destroyed by incautious, or malicious use of the technology?

"Today we have seen just a minor taste of what can happen when the technology escapes control. This is why I have dedicated my life to the protection of the whole earth from this inevitable technological change. It cannot be stopped, but it can be controlled.

"But physical destruction is just the tip of the iceberg. Privacy and private property are gone—unless I uphold them! I did not take on this job lightly.

"The technology of teleportation exists. I hold it. I control it. And under my hand, the wealth and safety of the world will blossom. In these few months, there are many people who can testify to that.

"Those who attempted to wrest that control away from me would stop at nothing—they used neurotoxins, and explosives, and bullets and chemicals designed to destroy parts of my brain.

"I am proud to say that I have hurt no man. Officer Hobert was injured because I was attacked and taken out of action. Ngarta Habre, who attacked First Agent Archer, was detained for some time and is currently free, on the road in Brazil according to last accounts.

"During the rescues of myself and my agents, several law enforcement agents of various nationalities and types were also detained and will shortly be released. None of them have been harmed.

"I ask world opinion to judge me by my actions, not by the irrational fears of those who fear to lose their power.

"I am Emperor. I have a job to do—to preserve the safety of humanity while phasing in this new technology, and I cannot relinquish this duty.

"So today, reluctantly, I must take steps to see that the Empire is preserved."

He picked up a hand-held computer.

"All nations who participated in the arrest of my agents will have their first year's imperial tax taken in full, as of..." he tapped a key "...now. One billion dollars US equivalent has now been removed from the gold repositories of those nations.

"As for the poison attack on the Emperor, a penalty of ten billion dollars is additionally levied against the United States of America for permitting its agent, Admiral Forsythe to take such an action.

"In addition, the sovereignty of the US will be impaired for one calendar year. As of today, your borders are no longer in your full control. Fifty personal transportation spheres will open and close in random locations between cities of the US and other cities of the world.

"I take this action knowing full well that additional security measures will be necessary to contain the hazards of crime and terrorism that will be facilitated by this open border policy. I urge the US to act wisely, and humanely, and to remember this when another rogue agency decides to attack the Empire."

He set the little computer down.

"When I first spoke to the UN, I said that nations friendly to the Empire would be treated well. Keep that in mind.

"Due to a sudden surplus of gold in our vaults, and the need for the Empire to be more visible on the world stage, we are entertaining bids for the construction of several palaces or consulates in nations recognizing the legitimacy of the Empire.

"Additionally, the Empire will be constantly expanding the scope of our operations. Additional agents and employees of various skills will be needed. Advertisements will be placed in the newspapers. Job locations will be arbitrary, but imperial work facilities will be built in nations recognizing the Empire and providing diplomatic protection for our people.

"In summation, the Empire of Earth is real. It will stay and do its job. No man need fear us. No friendly nation need worry about our power. But the hand that takes up arms against us will fail."

The speech had obviously taken a lot out of the Emperor, and as he rolled his chair back, his doctor was already at his side, checking his pulse.

James walked forward. He could see Oriel working the concealed controls that manipulated the loud speaker.

"This concludes the imperial announcement," he told the audience of millions behind the cameras. "Various members of the imperial party will be available for interviews for as long as this portal is open."

Just then, a pair of fighter jets screamed in and suddenly vanished. One of the cameramen gasped.

James grinned, "Oh, don't worry about them. They've just suddenly found themselves a few hundred miles off course."

He stepped forward, and flickered over to the news crew.

"Now, who would you like to interview first?"

136

A day of talking to reporters was draining. James handled the scheduling.

His father gave one interview, but it was short. Diana gave three, to different news organizations. CNN had opened its doors to several competitors, and one at a time, James permitted one person to come through the portal after someone else left.

Four people at a time, max. And James checked the newcomers carefully for concealed weapons.

He even gave an interview himself, after turning his controls over to Oriel. It took at least two of them to monitor the skies for incoming planes and helicopters and to keep them at a safe distance.

"I miss football. It was a big regret that I wasn't able to complete my junior season due to an automobile accident ...

Riches? Well, I guess so. But you have to understand that I'm no longer living in Texas. My needs are different now. What good would a fancy sports car do for me now, when I can go anywhere instantly? ... Our family has always been strong. Even when the recent events separated us, I always had confidence in my parents, and I hope they have had confidence in me. ... A girlfriend? Hmm. Nobody in Texas at least."

Oriel gave an interview too. It was all in French, too fast for him to follow.

Various agents were interviewed. Once their hazard bonus made known, the most common questions were how they intended to spend their money, and what they thought of the Emperor.

"I believe that was the last interview." James widened the portal back to the CNN studio. "If you will please move the equipment back through."

By the time that was done, his parents and the doctor were gone. Oriel and Archer were handling the job of getting the various imperial agents home.

James assisted, escorting two of them himself.

Then, he popped back to the mountain where the interviews had been held.

It was approaching sunset. Helicopters were much closer now.

"Is anyone still here?" he shouted. But there was no one.

He retired to the base.

"Hi, Mom. How did it go?"

She was still dressed in her imperial gown, sitting in the chair by the computer screen. "My feet are killing me. I began wishing for a wheel chair of my own. The next time we hold a press conference, I want it to be in a nice indoor setting, with comfortable chairs."

"How is Dad?"

"He's back in bed. I've sent Dr. Feldstein back. Are you up to monitoring the board? I need to change."

"Go for it."

She got up and he took the chair. "Have you seen Oriel?"

"Yes, she was helping to get our agents home."

He nodded. She should be done with that before long.

James felt good. The world had a much better image of them. *We're real people, and we care about the safety of the world, but it's useless to try to stop us.*

137

"May I help you, *Madame?*"

The old lady was stepping across the uneven rock surface very carefully, using her cane. On her, the dove gray uniform looked a little ridiculous. Oriel remembered her name, Hilbert. Mrs. May Hilbert.

"Oh, you're that French girl, Oriel? I'm sorry to be a bother. I've just had a few falls in my time and it makes me nervous."

"You don't need to come down. Just stay where you are, and I can transport you home directly."

"Oh, that would be nice."

Oriel stepped up beside her, checking her list. The locations were pre-loaded into her watch. James had said to only use the hand controller, but she was getting used to working her watch buttons surreptitiously. She could cross her wrists and do it while her sleeves hid the action.

She stepped through the locations. Hilbert was number 12. "Are you ready?"

"Any time, Dear."

The sphere enveloped them and Oriel was ready to steady her as they moved two time zones east.

She stayed at Mrs. Hilbert's side as she walked to her front door and paused.

"Oh. I'm so sorry."

"What is it?"

The old lady looked ready to cry. "I must have left my purse back on the mountain. My keys are in it. This old brain has more holes in it than Swiss cheese."

Oriel patted her shoulder. "I'll go get it *en un éclair*!" She tapped the return button.

There it is. The long shadows showed the handle of the handbag. She picked it up and selected Hilbert's address again.

As she stepped into the Eastern Time Zone, the dart struck her side before she had time to turn around.

"So sorry my dear," was the last thing she heard before everything went black.

138

James called out, "Oriel? Are you back yet?"

He got up from his chair, and walked over to the 'kitchen', actually just an alcove with chairs, a table, and a refrigerator.

His parents were both there, shorn of their uniforms and looking normal again. "Have you seen Oriel?"

"No. Have you checked with Archer?"

James nodded. "I'll do that." He trotted back to the console.

"No," said Archer, his voice a little weak through the monitor portal. "I saw her a couple of times as we were moving people off the mountain, but not after that. Is there a problem?"

"Thanks. I don't know." He closed the connection.

His father wheeled up to the other console. "It's 'ParisWatch' isn't it?"

"Yes." James moved over to see what his father was doing.

He chose the location and brought up a watch monitor screen. The image was black.

James pointed to an info window.

It was listing each button as it was being pushed. The words were popping up quickly: **MODE ADJUST LIGHT MODE MODE ADJUST LIGHT LIGHT.**

Bob said, "That's not her. Someone else has her watch."

Someone was trying to find the combination to get through to them.

Bob clicked the ERASE PROGRAM button, as James yelled, "Stop!"

But it was too late. Oriel's watch was just a watch.

"Dad! That's her only way back! She needed that watch."

"We can't risk it."

James stared at the screen, wishing the monitor window would pop back up, but the ERASE PROGRAM had completely detached all connections to her watch.

"Let's get her location back. It's in the logs."

His father, looking worried too, nodded.

They opened a free-floating monitor just a few feet from the last known location. It was still black.

"Move it around." His father complied.

The watch appeared to be in a blacked out room in an office building. There were several men in the corridors and neighboring offices. They all wore black suits.

"We didn't get them all. Forsythe's agents." Diana had come to watch over their shoulders.

They checked carefully for Oriel. There was no sign of her.

"No." James was anxious, fighting the urge to pull the controls away from his father. "We need to see what's going on in that black room."

His father opened a command line window and started typing fast. "This monitor is on camera B12. I'll switch it over to the E-bank. Those cameras have infra-red capabilities."

The black window blinked, and a green, noisy image replaced it. A man stood alone holding the watch in his hand. He was pressing buttons. He winced when he pressed the **LIGHT** button. James could see light leaking out around the man's night goggles every time he did that.

"Where is Oriel? She's not here."

Diana pointed to something on the screen and her husband nodded.

"What?" asked James.

"He's got all kinds of weapons strapped to him. If he had gotten in here..."

James could see it now. It was a nightmare version of a soldier going into battle. Some were guns. Others had to be bombs.

"Open a little window. I can grab the watch out of his hand before he can react."

"Too dangerous. It's just a watch."

"Mom! It's important. As long as they think the watch is a special device, they're still in the dark. We can't let them keep it."

He turned to his father, "Dad. I can do this. You handle the controls. Open and shut. Just one second."

Bob Hill stared at his son for a long moment.

"It's dangerous."

"It's something I have to do." Part of him knew it was a risk. *But it's Oriel's watch!*

"Okay."

"Bob," objected his wife.

"Step back away from the computers. Get a good stance."

"Dad, I'm the athlete in this family." He did as he was told. He braced his legs, and cocked his arm.

His father positioned a ten-inch sphere right in front of him. "I'll move the remote portal in five, four, three, two, one."

The sphere turned dark. James jabbed his hand in, felt the touch of skin and plastic. He grabbed the watch and jerked it out.

There was a blast, like a cannon shot. His hand stung, and he was thrown to the gravel floor.

"Ouch ouch." It hurt.

Diana was there in an instant, muttering "Oh my, oh my" and grabbing his arm.

"What happened?" asked his father.

"It burns." James looked at his hand, flexing the fingers. All the hair on the back of his hand was burned off.

Diana checked it carefully. "Superficial burns. I'll get some ointment." She got up.

James eased to his feet and picked up the watch. It seemed okay. "What happened on the other side?"

Bob was working the controls. "Just a second. The blast took out that camera."

A second portal showed two floors of that building damaged. There were bodies that didn't move. In the distance, sirens could be heard.

"We're lucky. The portal had started to collapse when the shock wave hit."

"But what happened? I didn't do anything but grab the watch."

His father held out his hand. "Let me see it."

James handed it over.

Experienced hands checked it out. "Here. There is a loop of fine wire around the pin that holds the band in place. They rigged it to explode if their assassin ever lost the watch."

Diana said, "Hold out your hand." She started working the ointment in.

James asked, "But why?"

Bob shrugged, "Either they really didn't want him to lose it, or else they expected us to retrieve it and wanted to cause the most possible damage to us when we did.

"They almost succeeded."

His hand was burning again, like the muscle rub after a workout.

Diana asked, "How long has Oriel been missing?"

"An hour, at the most."

Bob said, "This was well planned. It can't have been thrown together in minutes. It was a kidnapping, not a lucky break for them."

"Another bad agent?"

"Who did Oriel take home?"

James said, "Check the logs."

139

Oriel struggled to shake off the blackness, but her head ached, and there was this constant whine.

"She's awake." It was a strange voice, yet familiar.

"Mes maux de tête. Que continue ici?"

"Speak English. We know you can."

A woman was leaning over the back of the seats in front of her. *Je suis dans un avion.* Why was she in an airplane?

"Who are you?"

The woman let her pistol show in her hand. "You don't recognize me?"

The voice was familiar. "Mrs. Hilbert?" This was no old lady. No older than her mother at least.

"Not really. We've got the real Hilbert on ice. I'm just the substitute you rescued instead. Oh, but its good to be out of those wrinkles!"

Oriel tried to raise her arm, but she was shackled. Chains connected her wrists to an iron ring in the floor.

Ma montre-bracelet est allée.

The faux-Hilbert said, "Missing your wrist-watch? We have it. With luck, our man is already in your base, and shutting down your short-lived empire.

"We knew it had to be the wrist-watch. My lovely gold pendant was just a ruse, we know that.

"That Kurt Sommer was an idiot. Our organization is a bit more sophisticated. You never knew we had the pendant x-rayed and checked out, did you? It had to be the watch, that lovely Lady's Rolex Oyster quartz your people handed out like party favors at the rescue."

She displayed it proudly on her wrist. "The lab boys couldn't keep it long, not when you were using it to keep tabs on me. They didn't think it did anything.

"Ah, but your watch! I saw what you did. Press a few buttons and blip across the continent. What a lovely way to get out of a dull meeting." She showed her teeth.

Oriel let her babble. Just wait until James pulled her out of here! Then this dull person would see who was stupid.

"Oh, in case you are expecting to be rescued, don't hold your breath. We know what your weakness is. We studied hundreds of reported teleportation events. Every one was stationary location to stationary location. You can't teleport from a moving location.

"And this," she tapped the wall. "This is a C-141B Starlifter, with in-flight refueling already scheduled. We can keep you moving forever. Your Emperor can do nothing to save you."

Oriel scowled. *My James will come for me.*

140

They're right. James looked at the monitor window locked to the quartz oscillator in the fancy watch. Oriel was moving at nearly 400 miles per hour. If he stuck his hand through a portal to her, it would be ripped off. If they pulled her out, she would still be traveling at jet aircraft speeds.

Nothing but sound and light could get through.

Bob muttered, "She is talking to us."

"What?"

His father shook his head. "She's not really talking to Oriel. Why would she tell her all that detail?"

"To scare her. She's a nasty mean lady and likes to scare people."

"No. If they wanted to scare her, a vulnerable little French girl, they would get one of those big goons to do it, not a woman.

"And the details. Some of it means nothing to Oriel. Why did they tell her the exact type and model of plane? It's so we will know they aren't bluffing.

"They've got her trapped, and we can't get her free. When they find out their assassin failed, they will tell us their ransom demands."

James nodded. Dad was right. They would attempt to trade Oriel for access to the teleportation controls.

It was unthinkable. These were the same people who poisoned Dad, and were ready to destroy his mind. It would be evil of the worst kind to give them this power.

But he couldn't leave Oriel in their hands. What kind of backup plan did they have for her? Torture her on the plane while they could do nothing but watch?

I could kill them all, except for the pilot. It would be easy. There were a dozen ways. *But to what extent are they willing to go?* That assassin trying to get into the base knew he was a human bomb.

Would this group just crash the plane for spite? Until the plane was stopped, they could do nothing, and the black-suits would put a bullet through Oriel's head before they lost that edge.

He looked at his father. The man's face was drawn. For just a few hours, up on the mountain in the sunlight, he had looked good. Now the stress had all come back.

Dad won't trade for Oriel. He can't. It would kill him, but he probably couldn't even trade for me if I were in her place. One life in exchange for the safety of the world—it was an impossible burden.

"I'll just have to rescue her."

The Emperor asked, "How?"

"I don't know yet. But I will, or die trying."

141

Diana called from her computer terminal, "The real Mrs. Hilbert is in Philadelphia."

James walked over to look.

She was searching through records. "Here it is. They put her in the psychiatric wing under the name 'Ruth Lamby'. She supposedly has delusions that she is an Imperial agent."

James nodded, "We'll get her out."

Bob said, "Wait until I check for bombs! And we can't bring her here. Not now. It's too risky."

James headed for his terminal. "I'll call Archer."

"It is all my fault," May Hilbert wept, once they transferred her to one of Archer's seaside houses.

Empress Diana poured her a cup of tea. "Nonsense. Evil people don't need you taking responsibility for their actions."

She sniffed. "But it is. When the Emperor stopped taking my reports, I was afraid. They were talking about arresting people on the television and I was afraid it would destroy my daughter to see me arrested. I called the police, and those men in black suits came and got me.

"If I hadn't weakened...."

Diana said, "They would still have come for you. They were very efficient at locating our agents."

She looked at the elderly lady with sadness. "We should not have put you in this position, and I hope you will believe we would never have left you trapped like you were if we had known about it."

She sniffed again. "That hard woman. She visited me and mocked the way I talk. She pretended to be me?"

"Yes. We just now discovered the truth.

"Don't worry. First Agent Archer here will get you a safe place to live and contact your family."

Diana made her goodbye and whispered to Archer, "Take care of her, but make sure she sees nothing. As of now, she's retired. I'm sure she's innocent, but she weakened once. We can't afford it again."

142

James moved his flying eye all through the plane, locating the crew and the black-suits. The cargo/troop transport wasn't outfitted with elaborate spy cameras or anything like that. From everything he could tell it was just a plane somehow borrowed from a National Guard unit.

Oriel was crying. It wrenched his heart inside. He moved his viewport directly in front of her face. She gave a gasp, and he moved it.

One of the guards got up and checked on her.

Oriel blinked the tears from her eyes and glared at him.

James looked the situation over. *I could get the shackles off of her, just like I removed Mom's handcuffs.* As long as both sides of the portal were in the plane, flying at the same speed, there would be no problem.

"No!" cried Oriel as the guard injected her with something. "No." Her voice drifted off. They had drugged her again.

"Dad! Can we get a jet plane of our own, and fly beside this one? We could pull her across."

His father sighed, "In a perfect world, yes. But we don't have a plane. I thought of that. We would have to hijack a plane and a crew. They would have to be in the same part of the world as the C-141, because of the curvature of the earth. We would have to trust that the pilot wouldn't try something crazy, and we can't, because we would be the hijackers.

"If only we had a friendly country, with an airforce, we might be able to try it."

James said, "We're running out of time."

Bob snarled, "I know!"

Something jelled.

"Dad. I know how to do it!"

"Tell me."

"The curvature of the earth!"

Power

143

"No. It's much too dangerous." His father shook his head. Diana had the same expression.

"Mom, Dad, since when has this family taken the safe road?"

"Dad, you risked your life becoming the Emperor. You had to, to prevent a greater evil. I demand the same right! I will not let them destroy Oriel, and I won't let you take the guilt for not giving in to them.

"Dad, it's all the same evil."

His mother looked at her husband's face. She could see him weakening. "You'll die," she cried to James.

"No I won't. Dad will be driving."

"But how will you stop?"

"Simple. Africa."

144

They couldn't steal a plane, but James had no problem stealing a high-altitude pressurized flight suit. It was made for a fighter pilot. Finding bottles of aviator oxygen weren't much harder to find. He left a stack of imperials by the locker.

"James." The voice sounded in his ear, the headphones were connected to his MP3 player so that Dad could lock onto the circuitry.

"Yes Dad."

"I've done the math. The mid-air refueler tanker plane has taken off. It's an HC-130, from the same National Guard base the C-141 came from. Its max speed is 289 miles per hour, so they will have to drop down to at least that amount while they are refueling. But that's still a higher velocity than a trained skydiver can reach."

"You'll just have to take me higher. With less atmosphere, and less drag, I can go faster."

"Yes, you can go faster, but if we teleport her out of her seat into a windstorm at 300 miles per hour, she's likely to be torn apart. Even if she were conscious, it might be too violent. She could have her neck snapped before you could do anything."

"She's still unconscious?"

"Looks like it."

"Let's hope she wakes up soon. If they refuel, it'll be another ten hours before we can get anywhere near this close."

145

"Oriel. Oriel. Can you hear me?"

She struggled against the drug-textured blackness.

"Oriel, wake up. James is coming to get you."

James, mon joli. Où êtes-vous allé?

The black closed down again.

146

James fell fast. A sphere had dropped him off in mid-air 40,000 feet above the Pacific Ocean. It was his first skydive, and it was much harder to control his arms and legs than it had appeared in the movies.

The web page had said that maximum speed could be reached falling either head down or toes down. James struggled to hold himself rigid.

It was a strange surreal place. The sky above and the ocean below blended together in the haze of distance. There was no solid object within miles. Only the reddish glow of dawn on the horizon gave him any sense of direction.

As he dropped, the wind noise grew outside his helmet.

"Refueling has begun. They are down to 260 miles per hour, heading east, just like their pilot projected. How are you doing James."

"I don't know. What's my speed?"

"Pretty close."

"Oriel?"

"Son, it doesn't seem like she hears me."

"Then you'll have to put me inside."

"What? I can't do that!"

"It'll work. Blow their cabin air. Distract them long enough to for me to get her. I can keep her oriented against the wind."

There was silence. "Dad?"

"Okay, but I'll have to tune your velocity vector. Now moving you up 9000 feet and south 300 miles."

The sky changed around him. He could feel himself speeding up slightly.

147

"Oriel! Wake up now. Oriel, James is coming."

The noise in her head was getting most insistent.

She tried to blink, but the light was blurry.

"Oriel!"

"*Oui,*" she muttered.

"Oriel, can you hear me?"

She couldn't put her thoughts together.

"Oriel, in just a few seconds, your shackles will come off. When that happens, curl up into a ball. A tight little ball. Can you hear what I'm saying?"

148

The curvature of the earth. Dad had said that all the teleport gates were controlled from a single point, and that's where they were oriented. The control matrix was locked to the ground, rotating with the earth. That's why you could step from Texas to France without feeling their very different velocities. With respect to the rotating controller, there were no different velocities.

But the same rotating framework meant that a skydiver falling straight down at 260 miles per hour over the Pacific Ocean could exactly match a C-141 transport cruising east over Kentucky.

James heard his father's count down. "Five, four, three, two, one."

The limitless sky over the vast featureless ocean suddenly switched with the chaos of a transport in the midst of rapid decompression. Dust and papers were blowing through the cabin as a basketball sized sphere let the pressurized air escape. A klaxon was blaring emergency. And two sets of pilots suddenly realized that connected by the fueling boom, they could both be torn apart.

James was on the floor, down suddenly at his back. He looked to the side.

Oriel! She was folding herself up into a ball, her eyes wide with terror. Shackles were on the ground.

James grabbed her arm. Their eyes locked.

She lunged towards him. He could see her mouth forming his name.

"Dad! Now!"

A hurricane torrent blasted them. James pulled her close. He folded her head against his chest, trying to shield her against the wind.

Her arms were tight around him.

"Aieee!" she was shrieking, and the sound was getting louder.

The wind was easing.

In his head, his father called, "James! James can you hear me?"

"Dad. I'm fine. We're both out."

It had been dawn over the Pacific. It was now sunset over the sands of the Sahara, and they were falling upwards.

"James?" Oriel called to him, but inside the helmet, it was hard to hear her.

"James," said his father, "You are approaching zero velocity. Five, four..."

James held his gloved hand before her face, pulling in fingers in count with his father's voice.

"Three, two, one."

There was a flicker, and the two of them were teleported to the ground. They fell to the sand from a height of three feet.

149

"James! James are you down okay."

"Fine, Dad." He pulled the helmet off and jerked the earphones free.

"Are you okay?" he asked.

Oriel lay in the sand, her new uniform torn in places by the wind. She nodded. "You will explain to me sometime what happened?"

He unzipped one of the numerous outside pockets on the flight suit. "Here. I got your watch back."

She took it, and pulled him down in the sand with her.

James could hear the faint sound of his father's voice as he felt himself drift away into the bliss of her kisses and the softness of her arms.

150

There was an earthquake. Their kiss broke apart and a pile of sand engulfed them.

"Oh no you don't," said the Emperor. "I know how Bond movies end as well as you do. But it's not over yet."

James felt his face flush as he pulled himself up.

Dr. Feldstein moved quickly to Oriel. "No, you just stay put young lady. You've been drugged. Let me check your blood pressure."

Diana gave her son a big hug. "I'm proud of you," she whispered.

James walked closer to the computer screens. "What's happening, Dad?"

He looked worried. "The HC-130 lost its fueling boom when the C-141 started to dive because of the air loss. I think the tanker will make it back okay, but the C-141 sustained damage to its fuel system. It is losing fuel by the gallons. Whether it makes it to an airfield or not is anyone's guess."

151

Emperor Robert looked tired and angry on the TV screen.

"Just yesterday, at my press conference, I had hoped that it would be weeks, perhaps months, before I had to appear before you again. But it wasn't to be.

"No more than fifteen minutes after the last of the interviews, agents of Admiral Forsythe of the United States, kidnapped and drugged our first French agent, Oriel Meirieu.

They then attempted a raid on my base of operations, intending to kill all of the royal family. When that raid aborted due to our security precautions, a suicide bomb destroyed their office building in East Philadelphia. I am sure local forensic experts will confirm that it was their own bomb that killed those agents."

He paused and looked to his side. The camera zoomed back to include Oriel standing at his side in a fresh uniform and with her hair touched up.

"We are very proud to report that our Oriel Meirieu was rescued with no injury from a military transport craft flying over Kentucky. She had been drugged and shackled and kept in the plane. The rogue agents had foolishly supposed that we could not teleport to a moving target.

"Unfortunately, the two aircraft used by them were damaged during the rescue. No one was killed, but the kidnappers have been removed to imperial custody."

He pulled up the same pocket computer he had used the day before.

"These attempts cannot go unpunished." He pressed a key. "An additional two billion in gold is assessed from the United States for this attack. Will you people please get your house in order?"

152

Rudy Ghest sat on a rock in the shade and played Mancala with FBI agent Wilson, who had become something of a celebrity when he started teaching the game to all comers. Needing no props other than some pebbles and pits in the ground, it was a perfect way to kill time on the island.

Rudy had taken the seat that gave him a good view of the Admiral's gathering ground. A number of people sat nearby. Once the initial scouts had reported that the Exit cavity in the giant stone ball did nothing, quick escape dropped off the top of everyone's agenda. The top three interests now were gossip, surveillance, and food.

The food was at least plentiful, but the UN food biscuits were bland. Two of their number, one of Admiral Forsythe's spooks and a German Verfassungsschützer agent could be counted on to provide fresh fish for every meal, and it was starting to become a contest between them who could provide the best catch.

Secrets were a prime item of trade, along with spare bullets. Rudy now knew far more about Admiral NoBadge than he cared to. Thus the surveillance.

Admiral Forsythe had never stopped being on the job. The first thing he did after consolidating his group was to hold long serious talks with certain others on the island. Frequently, the grapevine would pinpoint the other man as a former or current spook with a dark past.

Rudy took it as quite a compliment that the Admiral paid him no attention at all.

He glanced at his watch, still keeping perfect New York time even after his dunk in the ocean. 5:59 PM. It was about time.

He looked over to a wide spot on the beach. People were clearing the spot.

At the top of the hour, a large sphere flickered into existence thirty feet up filled with yellow food packages. It quickly vanished, leaving the food to crash down on the beach. The surrounding troops moved into to stack them and begin the day's meal preparation.

An amplified female voice caught everyone's attention.

"Since you are all here, it is now time to bring you up to date."

The camp stopped in its collective tracks. Those sitting down rose to their feet.

"This is Empress Diana. You are a collection of people who, for various motives, have conspired against my husband. You were removed here to get you out of the way during a critical phase in the history of the Empire.

"Once you reach civilization, you can find out the details, but be advised that several nations, including one permanent member of the UN Security Council, have recognized the Empire, granting full diplomatic standing for ourselves and our agents.

"As many of you are from the United States, be advised that a proposed declaration of war on the Empire was soundly defeated by congress.

"Now before I tell you how to get home, I have a personal message from me to you:

"If anyone attempts to hurt my husband again, or any of his agents, know this, I will have complete control of the power of the Empire, and I will be much, much less forgiving than he has been."

Rudy glanced at the Admiral, whose face looked like a storm front.

Empress Diana's voice became more cheerful.

"This island was designed, not as a prison or place of punishment, but as storage facility, to delay the actions of our enemies. As such, there is a way out, one that we have temporarily deactivated.

"You have no doubt located the Exit chamber and discovered the selector and the button. As of this moment, it is now active. You may choose a continent as your destination and push the button. One person at a time in the chamber, or it will not work.

"You cannot choose a destination more specific than a continent. A location will be chosen randomly, but you can count on appearing on dry land at ground level.

"The only previous inhabitant of the island successfully made his escape to South America, and is currently hitch-hiking his way to Rio.

"Now, unless you have a deathwish, I advise you to avoid Antarctica, the chances of you appearing anywhere near a settlement are extremely slim.

"That's it. Choose a continent and make your own way home from there. Consider it a 'trial by ordeal'. Those of you with survival skills training may wish to coach the others before you leave. Those considering waiting until more conventional help arrives should think again. Even if the island is discovered, no plane or ship will be able to approach it."

For the first time, Rudy was able to sense some fear in the Admiral. What is it? That he won't be able to take his goon squad through the gate with him, or that he will have to trust his fate to the man he tried to kill?

153

"Your father has made it clear to me that I should not try to seduce you." Oriel smiled bewitchingly. The lights on the Eiffel Tower highlighted her eyes. She was wearing the dress that put three deadly agents on the floor.

"Oh?" James asked. "And why is that?"

"He says that you have much education to complete, and you have not the maturity to handle your duties and an impulsive young wife at the same time. Bah!" She dismissed the argument with a wave of her hands.

"I think your father has plans to seduce the British into acknowledging the Empire with a royal alliance. There are many unattached females among the Windsors I think."

James smiled. "Oh, I don't think that would work. Besides there's a little Texas cheerleader that has already expressed some interest in me."

Oriel's eyes glittered, "And what might this one's name be?"

He laughed, "I would fear for her life if I told you, but you needn't worry. She was crass and unsophisticated, and I haven't given her an instant's thought since I met you."

He watched her pull her claws back in, and compose her face. He asked, "How did your interview go, that day on the rock? I've reviewed it, but when you Parisians talk to each other, the words blend together, and I can't make sense of it all."

Oriel smiled at the memory.

"Oh, I was very open and clear. We French are very businesslike about these things. I told them that it would be a great shame if the imperial palace were to be built in some cultural backwater. I said the Empire would soon eclipse the importance of nations, and it would be very important for France to become a formative influence on the current royal family, and for its generations to come."

James checked the surroundings. It was habit. The invisible bullet-bouncing spheres encircled them, but he wasn't quite comfortable being out in public. Camera flashes occurred so frequently that he had begun to tune them out.

"Well, you must have been very persuasive. France's official recognition has been the breakthrough we needed. Although, I had chalked it up to the French glee at seeing the United States get its hands slapped."

"Oh, we are not so petty, just practical, very practical." She reached across the table and joined hands with him.

154

Rudy Ghest climbed the ladder, grateful he was midway through the group, and that it had been rebuilt and anchored against the rock. He stepped into the chamber and looked at the crude selector dial.

His assignment was in North America, but towns were much closer together in Europe. Besides, the US might not have its welcome mat out for people arriving by teleportation, especially if there had been enough resentment to attempt a declaration of war.

He moved the little arrow to Europe, and with a glance out to the ocean visible in the distance, he pressed the red button.

And appeared in someone's office.

"Have a seat Mr. Ghest."

He glanced quickly around the room. No guards.

He settled into the chair, amazed at how much better cushions felt than rocks.

"James Hill, I presume." He had seen the pictures, and since the 'Empress Diana' had spoken, it had settled who the identity of the Emperor firmly enough.

James nodded, "Although I am told that I must get used to 'Crown Prince James' from now on.

"I apologize for interrupting your trip home, but I wanted to have a talk with you in private."

Rudy nodded. Let the man talk.

"You must be aware, that teleportation removes all pretense of privacy. In our dire struggle when the Emperor was poisoned..."

Rudy looked up at that. That had been the rumor, but no one had admitted it.

"Yes, poisoned, by the man you identified as 'NoBadge' in your reports. In any case, I investigated everyone I could identify, including all the members of the FBI Emperor Task Force. I must say I was very impressed by what you wrote.

"Yes, your reports were read, you were observed secretly, the investigations from other agencies on you were tracked down and examined."

Rudy nodded. "Very impressive."

James shook his head. "Okay, for an amateur. Thus far, the Empire does not have a security agent that isn't an amateur. I would like to offer you the job of setting up a specialized security force with the goal of protecting the Empire, and when the time comes that others re-invent teleportation, of bringing other users under the rule of law."

"Which law?"

James spread his hands. "There is only one law controlling teleportation, the will of my father, the Emperor."

Rudy shook his head, "I already have a job."

"A good and honorable one, I am sure. In fact I am offering you one of two jobs. The Empire will need a liaison with Interpol as well. But I would much prefer you become the head of our security. I have reviewed this with my father, and we both agree that you are the man for the job."

Rudy was unsettled by the offer. He found something appealing about it.

"I'm not sure that I could be comfortable working for an absolute ruler. I have always believed in the rule of law over the rule of a man."

James nodded, "We are Americans—a little displaced now, but still Americans by culture. The whole idea of an Emperor, of a royal family, of a monarchy—it is difficult to absorb.

"Long ago, well before he invented the spheres, my father told me once that the best government was a monarchy, and the worst government was a monarchy. Solomon was the wisest of the biblical kings and expanded the wealth and prestige of his land without fighting wars. His son was an idiot who fragmented the land and lost the majority of its territory.

"Democracy, by whatever flavor, trusts statistics and debate over wisdom. But human nature still responds intensely to the image of the leader. How many times have we latched on to the flawed leader, just because something in us believes in him?

"At this point in history, we have the right man, my father, the Emperor.

"The Empire today has a goal, the safety of humanity. But in fifty years, or a hundred, the technology of teleportation will be absorbed and controlled and be no more dangerous than any other. When that time comes, what will the security forces of the Empire be doing? Spending all of their time and energy keeping the Empire in power, for power's own sake?

"If history is any guide, that's the way to bet.

"Rudy Ghest, do you think you could create a security force that could do better? Think about it. How would you institutionalize a sane and responsible force? One that when you are gone, will still look to humanity's own good?"

Rudy listened. The boy would be a powerful leader some day. It would be nice to be on that side.

"I can't jump ship."

James nodded. "I didn't expect you to, not yet."

He tossed Rudy a little box with a button.

"When you press it, you will be back on your journey home. Press it again, and we'll talk some more."

155

Papeete, Tahiti made a welcome new headquarters.

The High Commissioner of Tahiti quickly followed Paris in recognizing the Empire.

It was James who suggested that working in the sunshine was better for his health than inside a darkened cave.

Emperor Robert strode across the veranda of their newly acquired office building. They had several offices, a radar complex being constructed on the roof for defensive alerts, and a lovely glassed-in command and control center. All just a quarter mile from the marketplace.

We need several of these. The computer screens didn't have to be anywhere close to the real teleportation control hardware. *Maybe a dozen, spread out all over the world.*

A commando team could overrun this place in an instant, but it would do them no good. He held the password, and a tap on his wristwatch could shut it down in an instant.

No one can take over control now, except maybe James.

He smiled, *That's how it should be.*

A lean, serious young man in a gray uniform sat monitoring the status screen.

The Emperor put his hand on the back of the chair. "How are you doing, Joseph?"

The man looked up from his screens. "Sorry, your Majesty, I didn't hear you enter." He prepared to stand.

"Stand down, Joseph. I just wanted to see how the new software was working."

"Fine, sir ... sire."

"Oh drop the honorifics. Do you mind if I drive for awhile? Give you a break for a few minutes."

"Of course, your ... of course." Joseph stood, and turned over the chair to the Emperor. When the mouse began to fly over the screen, he realized he had been dismissed and left.

Bob watched him leave, and then activated a privileged control window.

Admiral Forsythe was the last man on the island, and after nearly two weeks alone, a spotter had seen him heading for the Exit.

Once he was gone, he could move the crew that kidnapped Oriel from their confinement inside one of the hundred foot tall cavities in the Himalayas to the island. If he could ever get an agreement with the United States, he would prefer to turn them over to the Philadelphia police along with evidence of their crimes.

I don't want to be both High and Low Justice. Let cities do what cities do, and nations do what nations do.

Being Emperor was a lot harder than he had imagined.

Bob glanced at the teleporter options. He could override the selector in an instant and drop the man into Antarctica, or the middle of the Pacific. His watch had picked up every word he had spoken. How many times had the man suggested that others nuke this base? How much blood was on his hands?

The Admiral was at the top of the ladder, and stepped into the exit chamber.

Every empire in history was built on blood. Every last one.

Forsythe set the selector for North America, but paused. He waited.

Can he sense me watching over him?

The mouse hovered over the options. Just a click would remove this threat to his family, and to the world.

He shifted his mouse away, just before the Admiral clicked and landed flat on his face in a blackland field in Alabama.

Maybe tomorrow, I'll have to do it. But not today. Not today.

156

James took a deep breath and said, "Dad, I can't go back to high school."

His father relaxed in the sun. The swim in the bay had done him a world of good. No one had noticed their arrival, so for the time, they could relax.

Dad had agents purchasing a number of secluded homes and resorts, most of them in friendly nations. No one could watch them all. Unlike any royal family before them, they could outrun the reporters.

"Explain."

James struggled to put his thoughts into words.

"Well, for one thing, I have a lot to learn. I need to learn things they don't teach in a school where every teacher is named 'Coach'. I've got a dozen languages to learn, politics, philosophy. I think I need to understand the theory of legal systems much better than I do now. And history. I need a ton of history."

"It sounds like a lot of work. Do you think you are up to it?"

"Oh yes. I have to, don't I? It goes with the job. It's just like football practice. Spend the time to get the results."

"Have you picked out a school?"

James swallowed. He didn't know how Dad would take it.

"Um. Several, actually. The thing is, they are in Europe. I can commute easy enough, but I'd rather avoid switching time zones all the time."

"So you would prefer to live over there?"

James nodded, with a grin. "It's not like you'll lose track of me. And it would make the languages easier to learn."

His father looked him in the eyes, "Paris, I assume?"

James felt his ears go hot.

"Well, yes. Oriel knows this apartment complex...."

"Just one thing, James."

"Yes, Dad?"

"Do you know who you are? Deep down inside, do you know who you are?"

James thought a moment. He had always thought he knew who he was.

A series of embarrassing memories flashed by. Who was that kid who only studied enough to stay on the team, and who was ready to be led on a merry chase by a pretty cheerleader?

Maybe he needed to have a nice, long, serious talk with Oriel. He knew her dream. She didn't try to hide it. And he had confidence that even if he decided to live in Texas, or Moscow, or Bombay, she would want to come with him.

But did she understand what his life would be? How it would have to be, with the lives of billions of people riding on him? She would have to, before they went too much farther.

He nodded to his father, the Emperor.

"Yes, Dad. I know exactly who I am."

"Then," he waved his hand, "you don't need me to tell you where you can live."

"I understand. Thanks Dad."

THE END

Small Towns, Big Ideas

Get all of these science fiction adventures by **Henry Melton**:

Emperor Dad	*Hutto, TX*
Roswell or Bust	*Las Vegas, NM*
Lighter Than Air	*Munising, MI*
Extreme Makeover	*Crescent City, CA*
Falling Bakward	*Chamberlain, SD*
Golden Girl	*Oquawka, Il*
Follow That Mouse	*Ranch Exit, UT*

Starting in the here and now, follow our young adult heroes as they step out of the ordinary and confront the fantastic. No matter where the story starts, no place in time or space is out of limits for these adventurers.

Contact **Wire Rim Books** or your favorite on-line book seller.

http://www.WireRimBooks.com

Roswell or Bust
by Henry Melton

Novel 6" x 9" Trade Paperback

List: 12.95 ISBN 978-0-9802253-0-3

The mute girl on the motorcycle was a refreshing change from Joe's work at the family motel, but a talking dog, Men in Black, and a 2000 mile road trip through the Southwest put him face to face with the strangest motel guests he'd ever seen.

Contact **Wire Rim Books** or your favorite on-line book seller.

http://www.WireRimBooks.com

Family Science Fiction
by Henry Melton

Anthology 6" x 9" Trade Paperback

List: 12.95 ISBN 978-0-9802253-3-4

There's more than just the lone wolf hero in science fiction, and from the pages of ANALOG and other magazines and anthologies, Henry Melton has selected some of his best tales where family is more than just an idle thought. Includes the gaming classic, *Catacomb*, and *The Christmas Count*, as well as several totally new stories.

Contact **Wire Rim Books** or your favorite on-line book seller.

http://www.WireRimBooks.com

Emperor Dad

by Henry Melton

A family tale for those who want to rule the world.

Novel 6" x 9" Trade Paperback

List 12.95 ISBN 978-0-9802253-4-1

What people have said about Emperor Dad:

"This book is awesome - adventure, humor, great ideas, and a fast pace. I couldn't put it down, and it's as good or better than Harry Potter - it has everything I look for in a book and more." Pat Downs

"I had a blast reading this book! With every page turned, you don't want it to end." J. Stock

"If you liked _Jumper_ by Steven Gould, you will love this book! ... Both books feature teleportation and governments trying to stop the teleporter; both feature interesting characters, just trying to make the best of a, well, weird situation. Both are a great deal of fun to read. " Pope Cahbet

Contact **Wire Rim Books** or your favorite on-line book seller.
http://www.WireRimBooks.com

Come enjoy other stories by Henry Melton at **http://HenryMelton.com** where you will find free short stories and pointers to other works.

Follow the extensive American and International travels of Henry and his award winning nature photographer wife Mary Ann Melton on their blogs:

Idle Thoughts
http://henrymelton.blogspot.com

Mary Ann's View
http://maryannmelton.blogspot.com

Want to read more books like this one? More are written—exciting tales about young people who take that extra step and find themselves in worlds of adventure and imagination. Ask your librarian or bookseller for help, or contact Henry Melton or Wire Rim Books directly through their websites.

Wire Rim Books: **http://WireRimBooks.com**
Henry Melton: **http://HenryMelton.com**

Printed in the United States
202536BV00002B/106-123/P